THE PROPOSITION . . .

"Reckon a two-buck quickie won't be of any use to a man in your condition, mister," the whore said. "You'll need the five-dollar treatment. Or I'll stay the night, if you wanna pay ten."

"I'll pay ten, lady," Edge answered, opening his eyes as lamplight spread across the room from where she stood at the bureau. As she came away, Edge was able to see his reflection in the mirror. The first time he had seen himself since long before Beth died.

"Lady, I wouldn't trust a man who looked like me," he growled, frowning at the gauntness of his features, the hollowness of his eyes, the ingrained dirt in the exposed flesh, and the irregular bristles that covered the rest of his face and his throat. Then he hardened his tone as she stopped by the bed and stooped to tug at one of his mud-caked boots. "Leave it!"

"What?" she answered, frightened at the latent cruelty that was abruptly visible on the surface of his eyes.

"I never even let Beth take my clothes off, lady."

"Who?" Her pleasant-looking features suddenly showed enlightenment. "Oh, it's a woman that's driven you to the bottle."

"Forget her, lady. That's what I'm trying to do."

"Pay me the ten and I'll do my damndest to help you."

WARNING

*This story is not for
the faint-hearted reader.*

S0-AVS-335

THE EDGE SERIES:

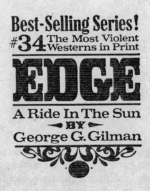

Best-Selling Series!

#34 The Most Violent Westerns in Print

EDGE

A Ride In The Sun

BY

George G. Gilman

PINNACLE BOOKS   LOS ANGELES

EDGE #34: A RIDE IN THE SUN

Copyright © 1980 by George G. Gilman

A Pinnacle Books edition, published by special arrangement with New English Library, Ltd.

First printing, July 1980

ISBN: 0-523-40865-X

Cover illustration by Bruce Minney

Printed in the United States of America

PINNACLE BOOKS, INC.
2029 Century Park East
Los Angeles, California 90067

For N. W., who rides even taller in the saddle than I do

A RIDE IN THE SUN

Author's Note

SINCE shortly after the first *Edge* book was published readers of the series have been writing to me. For the most part, I am happy to say, the mail has been highly complimentary about the books and, not unnaturally, I read such letters with great pleasure.

Several of them, however, did more than merely give a boost to my ego: the first one sowed the seed of an idea and those which followed caused this seed to germinate.

This process was begun when the *Edge* series was firmly established and the character of the man himself had made a strong impression on the readers. And not only Edge. The six troopers who rode with him throughout the greater part of the War Between the States seem also to have stayed in the minds of many readers after the books in which they appeared were set aside. In addition, certain other secondary characters in various stories have had a similar appeal.

What, readers have asked, was Edge like as a young man on the Iowa farm before the start of the Civil War? Why, others enquire, are there not more wartime stories featuring Sergeant Forrest, Bob Rhett, etc.? Edge's reaction to the untimely death of his wife was only touched upon in retrospect—cannot there be a story which covers this period of his life in detail?

In this book you are about to read, I have attempted to comply with these and other requests. In doing so, I have used almost the same technique I employed when writing the Civil War books—i.e. a running contemporary story broken by flashbacks to incidents in the past of Edge. I have departed from the technique insofar as each flashback takes the form of a complete short story: this has been made necessary because of the time that passes between the various incidents covered by the stories.

Of course, not every reader of the *Edge* series has written to me on general or specific points about the books, so I have no way of knowing the extent to which there is a desire to hark back over his past. I can but hope that every one of the many hundreds of thousands of people throughout the world who have read the previous books in the series will enjoy this one, and approve the technique I have used in writing it.

My thanks go to the readers who sowed the seed of the idea behind the book and to those who helped in the process of germination. I trust it will flourish.

Chapter One

OUTSIDE the Oro Blanco Cantina the mid-morning New Mexico sun beat down cruelly from a cloudless sky, glaringly bright and intensely hot, upon the cluster of adobe and frame buildings which comprised the inappropriately named border town of Paraiso.

Inside the cantina the temperature was maybe even higher. But at least the *patron* and his four customers did not have to squint against the harsh brightness of the day, unless they happened to glance out of the shaded interior toward the street beyond the single glassless window and the open door. They had no cause to do this, for there was nothing taking place beyond the confines of the cantina walls that was of greater interest than the poker game being played within them.

The game was five-card draw with nothing wild and the players were the quartet of Americans who sat around one of the four tables in the cantina. But the Mexican owner of the place was as eager to see the outcome of the game as the four players.

His name was Gomez and he stood at the end of the bar counter closest to the occupied table, in a position to watch the play and pass across uncapped bottles of beer whenever an order was signaled to him. He was a short, fat, almost bald man of about fifty with avaricious eyes and thick lips which he constantly wetted with the tip of his darting tongue. During the game, which was over two hours old, he was the only man in the cantina to alter the set of his fleshly features, expressing vicarious pleasure, disappointment or resignation at the swinging fortunes of successive hands.

The four players were a mixture of ages and builds but in general appearance they were representative of almost all the passing-through Americans who came to and quickly went from Paraiso.

Travis was a broad-shouldered, barrelchested, thick-waisted forty-year-old with a recently healed knife scar on his left cheek and the dead white skin of an ancient bullet wound across his right temple. The short clipped hair on his head was iron gray but his thick and drooping moustache was jet black. He spoke with a lazy southern drawl.

Wogan was a skinny Irish-American in his early thirties with a prominent facial bone structure, deep-set green eyes and the kind of animated Adam's apple that no poker player should have.

The youngest member of the quartet was Blackburn. He was about twenty, less than five and a half feet tall but powerfully built in proportion to his height; a good-looking young man, with soft brown eyes and a mouth that pouted. At the outset of the game he had told unfunny jokes between hands, but stopped when the laughter began to sound strained and the pots got bigger.

The fourth player had never laughed or even forced a smile at Blackburn's attempts to be funny. At six feet three inches, he was the tallest of the group at the table. His some two hundred pounds were stacked on lean lines, with not a single ounce of excess flesh to be seen. Although he spoke like a native-born American, and at first impression looked like one, he was able to talk to Gomez in accentless Spanish. A closer study of his face revealed unmistakable signs that there was some Latin blood in his veins.

It was the face of a man in his late thirties, yet the weathered flesh seemed to have too many lines that were too deep for a man of those years. In the dark coloration of the skin was the first clue to a heritage

4

drawn from a mixed marriage, for it was apparent that the hue had not been entirely as the result of exposure to the sun and the wind. The hair which framed the face was jet black, growing thick and long enough to brush the man's shoulders and conceal the nape of his neck.

There was also a trace of Mexican in the high cheekbones and the firm jawline, between which the dark, deeply lined skin was stretched taut. Maybe, also, in the cut of the hawklike nose and the wide, thin-lipped mouth—especially when the lips were curled back to reveal the white and even teeth in an infrequent smile, a smile that never injected a trace of warmth into his eyes: permanently narrowed under hooded lids, light blue and piercingly sage in the way they surveyed the other players, his cards, or perhaps a hungry fly that happened to alight on the table.

His eyes owed nothing to the part which a Mexican father played in his birth. They were the predominant feature he had inherited from his Scandinavian mother.

This player was the man who in recent years had been called Edge.

"Open for a hundred."

"Stay."

"Stay."

"Your big one and another."

"Fold."

"Shit, I'm out."

"Stay."

"Call."

Apart from Blackburn's weak attempts at humor between the earlier hands, talk at the table had been confined to asking for cards and playing them with, every now and then, the laconic exchange of poker terms interrupted by an equally curt request to Gomez for more beer.

The cantina's *patron* supplied what was needed and put the payments in a pocket of his leather apron with a smooth and mechanical series of actions, not needing to

5

shift his greedy gaze away from the pile of bills in the pot or the largest heap in front of the player who happened to be winning most at any particular time.

He hardly ever looked at the players themselves, and this not only because he found money far more interesting than men. For what was there to look at? Ten years he had owned and run the Oro Blanco Cantina in this godforsaken town in the south-west corner of New Mexico Territory, just a mile or so north of the border and about the same distance from the territorial line with Arizona. A town which existed for no other reason than as a stopover for men like these. All kinds of men, and yet really only two kinds: those who were running and those who were chasing them. They were outlaws and bounty hunters, coming north or going south, never lawmen. For if the fugitives reached this far north they were beyond the jurisdiction of the *Federales* and if they rode as far south as Paraiso, the United States peace officers had already given up the pursuit.

Gomez had seen a thousand or maybe even two thousand men like these four, dressed in dark-hued, hard-wearing pants and shirts with wide-brimmed hats atop their heads, carrying revolvers in tied-down holsters hung from well-stocked gunbelts. These were weary and wary-eyed men, with thick stubble on their faces and sweat-stained, dirt-streaked flesh and clothing, riding horses which were as tired and travel-marked as themselves, for it was a long way from anywhere to Paraiso.

One of the taciturn men at the table was different from the others and from the vast majority of cantina customers. The tall, lean man named Edge had come into town from the north two weeks earlier and had chosen to stay in Paraiso, renting one of the Oro Blanco's back rooms by the day. Sometimes that happened. But mostly Gomez's trade was drawn from men like Travis, Blackburn and Wogan who used the cantina for liquor and maybe food for an hour or so while they rested themselves and their mounts.

A card game among strangers met up in this way was

not unusual. But seldom was there so much money in a game. Gomez, who loved money with only slightly less fervor than life itself, knew that there was precisely $5,072 passing back and forth and moving around the table on this harshly hot morning in his cantina which smelled of stale sweat, old food and spilled liquor.

The largest share of this had been contributed by Travis, who rode into town early from the south. It was he who suggested a game of two-handed stud after the man called Edge finished eating breakfast. That had been pennyante stuff. The heavy money started to come out when Blackburn joined the game a few minutes after riding in from the north. A half hour later Wogan showed up in Paraiso, coming in off the same trail Blackburn had ridden. Travis invited the newcomer to take a hand and suggested the game be changed from stud to draw. So far he was close to $3,000 down, what he had lost divided about equally between the other three players. But he was as impassive in losing as Edge, Blackburn and Wogan were at winning, until a man rode up to the front of the cantina, dismounted, hitched his horse to the post outside and stepped onto the threshold. He stood there to allow his eyes to adjust to the shade inside the fetid, smoke-layered room.

"What the frig do you want, punk?" Travis snarled through yellow-stained teeth clenched to the small stub of an evil-smelling cigar. This after he had turned his head a fraction and his tiny eyes to the full extent of their sockets to glance away from the five cards in his hands to look briefly at the newcomer. "Either come in or move your friggin' ass outta here!"

It was the most he had said at any one time in the whole two hours since the game started. And he had never cursed before.

"Gee, what'd I do wrong?" the man in the doorway asked anxiously.

Blackburn and Wogan glanced at the newcomer without speaking and resumed study of their cards. Edge looked at him for a second longer and saw that he was a short, thin, sharp-featured kid of eighteen or

7

nineteen with a face sheened by sweat and clothes layered with trail dust.

"Mistimed your entrance on a high drama play, looks like," the half-breed answered evenly and returned his attention to the game, lifting two fifty-dollar bills from the pile in front of him and transferring them to the pot of opening bets.

"How the hell was I supposed to know?" the youngster growled resentfully as he crossed the threshold and moved to the center of the bar. "Like a beer."

Gomez scowled his displeasure at having to move away from the card game. Travis seated to Edge's left, Blackburn across from him and Wogan to the half-breed's right all stayed. Travis's temper was back under control. And Wogan's Adam's apple began to bob.

"Is there a guy named Josiah Hedges in town?" the youngster at the bar asked after the beer had been poured and Gomez extended a palm for payment.

"I have never heard the name, señor," the fat Mexican growled. "Twenty-five cents. Or I take pesos if you have come from Mexico."

"Who wants to know, kid?" Edge asked, the youngster's question having frozen him in the act of picking up more bills.

"Play the game or fold and jaw someplace else, mister," Travis snapped.

"My name's McCord," the newcomer said after taking a swig at his beer and smacking his lips in appreciation as the dust was washed from his throat. "But that don't matter. If this guy Hedges is around, I was told he'd pay for this beer and a lot more over the top."

"None of it friggin' matters, punk!" Travis snarled, and spat the stub of his cigar to the floor, where it came to rest among many others. "Because if Hedges is around Paraiso, he ain't in this stinkin' waterin' hole! Now, are you gonna bet or are you gonna yak, Edge?"

McCord did a double take at the halfbreed, his forehead creased by a frown. "Edge? Hedges? Maybe I didn't hear the name right."

Edge, his fan of cards laid face down on the table,

added two hundred dollars to the pot and fixed his narrow-eyed gaze on the puzzled face of McCord. "Somebody not saying it right is how it got changed, kid. Why should I buy you a beer and let you keep the change?"

The youngster smiled. "A lot more than the change, mister. Unless you give the bartender a hundred-dollar bill to break."

"Twenty-five cents somebody owes me," Gomez muttered and moved along the bar counter to resume his watch over the game.

"For what?" Edge asked as it was his turn to bet again, and he raised the ante to five hundred.

Each of the other three players eyed him with anxious suspicion after he had so casually added the money to the pot.

"A couple of guys give me a letter to deliver. Paid me twenty-five bucks for my trouble and reckoned as how you'd be sure to pay me a hundred after you got the letter."

Travis matched the half-breed's bet, Blackburn vented a low-voiced curse and folded and Wogan added to the pot after some stretched seconds of hesitation.

"Six hundred is how much it'll cost you fellers to stay in the game," Edge drawled, looking away from McCord for just long enough to count out the bills and drop them on the heap in the center of the table. "Let me have the letter, kid."

Now Travis took his time, switching his small-eyed gaze from his fan of cards to that of Edge and back again, as McCord came to the table, half-finished beer in one hand while the other delved in the front of his shirt.

"Shit, stay," Travis rasped, and used the back of a hand to brush sweat off his bullet-scarred forehead after placing his bet.

Wogan, his Adam's apple unmoving and a look of dejection on his thin face, merely sighed as he closed up his hand and placed the cards neatly on the deck.

McCord drew a small envelope from inside his shirt

as he halted at the table between Edge and Travis. The man with the scarred face grunted and ground his teeth together as McCord extended the letter toward the half-breed, but then jerked it back as a brown-skinned hand was raised to take it. "They said you'd give me a hundred bucks for it."

"After I've read it, kid," Edge answered evenly. But his slitted eyes, like slivers of blue ice between the lids, locked on McCord's eager gaze with a brief intensity that gave the lie to the half-breed's otherwise casual attitude.

McCord swallowed hard, then said, "How do I know you'll—?"

"I always pay what I owe, kid. Figure that in a town like Paraiso, won't cost more than ten dollars to bury you. Makes it the cheapest way to get what's mine."

McCord's nervousness increased when Gomez said, "I am mortician as well as *patron* of the cantina, *señor*. He is not very big, so I will do the job for seven fifty."

"This is gettin' to be a grave matter," Blackburn growled, then giggled.

Wogan grinned.

"I ain't gonna tell you again, Edge!" Travis rasped, and ran a shaking hand along his sweat-tacky brow. "Bet or I'll figure you've folded!"

"Seven," the half-breed murmured, put the bills in the pot and as part of the same movement swung his hand to the side, palm uppermost and fingers splayed. "Kid?" he asked without shifting his now impassive eyes away from the beaded, scowling face of Travis.

The envelope was placed in his hand and he folded his fingers over it and dropped it onto the diminished heap of bills in front of him. Travis pulled a cigar from a shirt pocket and clamped his teeth to it. He didn't light it. Now all attention was devoted to the card game and the only sounds in the cantina were of Travis's labored breathing and the shuffling footfalls of McCord as the youngster returned to the bar counter.

"Ante up or call, feller," Edge said softly, aware now that the big man's money was all on the table beneath his hands gripping the cards. A thousand dollars, give or take a few, which meant Travis had no alternatives to consider. Although Edge had only a few dollars in front of him, there was no way Travis could be certain this was the extent of his bankroll. So to raise the ante would force him to fold should the half-breed be able to cover and raise.

"Frig it!" Travis snarled, and bit through the cigar so that it fell, unlit, to the floor. "Call."

He pushed seven hundred dollars into the pot to make it worth $3,800. Then he joined everyone else except Edge himself in staring intently at the fan of face-down cards in front of the half-breed.

Edge looked at Travis, smelling the sweat of fear from the man's armpits and crotch as, with one hand, he scratched his right shoulder and used the other to move his five cards into a neat pile.

Then, "Ain't the best poker hand I ever had, feller," he murmured. "Lots can beat it."

He flipped the pile over and spread the cards. A five of diamonds showed first. Then the king of the same suit.

Travis sucked in some fetid air and began to alter his scowl into a grin." A lousy flush is—" he began, then froze.

The five of hearts came into view. Then the five of spades and of clubs.

"Four of a kind, feller," Edge said.

"Reckon you got yourself a full house, Travis," Blackburn rasped into the tense silence that followed the half-breed's words.

"Sure enough has to be that," Wogan added. "Only hand that beats a flush but don't top four of a kind."

Travis vented the air which was not released when his rising hopes were dashed. He opened his fingers so that his cards dropped to the table, two queens face up and the other cards hidden. Only then did he move his small eyes up from the winning hand to stare into the face of the winning man.

"You drew just one, mister," he said slowly and dis-

11

tinctly, as he hooked his fingers over the rim of the table. "Real lucky sonofabitch, ain't you?"

"Man makes his own luck lots of times, feller," Edge replied evenly. "Especially in a poker game."

Travis swung his head to glance toward McCord, who swallowed hard, licked his lips and took another swig of beer to empty his glass. When the small, hard eyes of the big man returned to examine Edge's face again, they saw that the half-breed's right hand was still busy scratching his shoulder.

"Even easier to get lucky with some outside help, ain't it? Open your letter, mister."

"Hey, I ain't nothin—" McCord began.

"Shut your mouth, punk!" Travis snarled.

"Beer, Gomez," Blackburn ordered.

"And another here," Wogan added.

Their tones were easy but, on the periphery of his vision, Edge could detect a trace of tension in their expressions and a rigidness in the way they sat on their chairs. He guessed they were open-minded about what was happening and were ready to lunge away from the danger area if there was a risk of getting hurt from trouble which did not concern them. But Travis had triggered a spark of suspicion in the backs of their minds. Edge was certainly the biggest winner and if he had cheated, then it was as much their business as Travis's.

"You're a bad loser, feller," the half-breed said as the Mexican bartender uncapped two bottles and passed them over the counter to Blackburn and Wogan. He shifted his hand and used the nail of a forefinger to scratch his throat just above the dull-colored beads strung on a leather thong around his neck. "Best you shut up your mouth or talk about something else. Either way, it'll just be money you're out."

Travis spat a stream of saliva from the corner of his mouth as Blackburn gave Gomez a dollar bill and said, "I'll buy."

"Need to know there's a letter in there, damnit!" the scar-faced man snarled.

12

He was left-handed. So it was his right which came up from the rim of the table and shot to the side, fingers clawed to snatch for the envelope in front of Edge, as the other one moved out of sight at the same speed.

Blackburn and Wogan had been careful to take the bottles in their left hands so that their rights were free to swing down and drape the jutting butts of their holstered Colts.

Edge's left hand had closed over the right wrist of Travis by then, holding it hard to the table over the letter among the money. His right was concealed for part of a second by the long hair at the nape of his neck. When it came into sight again it was fisted around the wooden handle of a straight razor.

"Gee!" McCord gasped.

Travis grunted as his attempt to rise was foiled by the strength with which the half-breed held his wrist trapped to the table. His chair tipped over backwards and his Remington came clear of the holster. But not before the long right arm of Edge had swung out across the table and started to arc back.

The Remington was above the table top, cocked but not leveled at the intended target.

Blackburn remained tensely in his chair. But Wogan went sideways out of his, lunging from the line of fire to come up hard against the front of the bar counter.

The honed blade of the razor sliced into the thin covering of flesh on the bone to the side of Travis's left eye. Both his eyes were closed in an involuntary blink as the half-breed's fist threatened them.

Off the bone, the blade dug deeper through the lid and into the ball. Travis screamed and half turned to put his back to Edge, but he could not jerk his wrist free. His gun exploded and the bills in the center of the table twitched and fluttered under the impact and in the slipstream of the bullet which cracked through them before thudding into the wall.

The blade cut a shallower furrow across the bridge of the nose, then sank deep again into the right eye.

"*Madre de Dios!*" Gomez gasped as he saw the cur-

13

tain of blood flood down over the fleshy cheeks of the big man.

The gun slipped from Travis's hand as Edge released his other wrist. The razor came clear of the flesh and the big man staggered away, raising both hands to his face and dragging his fingers through the warm stickiness of spilled blood. He screamed again, crashed into his overturned chair and pitched to the floor.

Edge used a dollar bill with a hole in it from the pot to wipe the blood from the blade before he replaced the razor in the leather pouch held at the nape of his neck by the beaded thong.

"You blinded me, you bastard!" Travis shrieked as he rolled onto his back, blood ozzing through the cracks in his fingers held to his face.

Blackburn and Wogan were as impassive as the half-breed and like him ignored the man on the floor to look down at the unopened letter.

Neither the gunshot nor the screams and desperate shouts of Travis had drawn an audience to the front of the Oro Blanco Cantina. For people who lived in a town like Paraiso were quick to learn that curiosity did not kill only cats.

"If you draw and aim those guns, use them," Edge said to the skinny Wogan and the good-looking Black-burn who continued to hold their right hands draped over holstered Colt butts. "Always try to warn people how I feel about having a gun pointed at me."

Neither man moved nor spoke for a stretched second. Then Blackburn raised the bottle to his lips and sucked beer from the neck as Edge picked up the envelope and used a forefinger to tear it open.

"Them guys told me there was a letter inside, mister," McCord said huskily.

"Somebody help me," Travis pleaded.

"Nobody's got eyes for you," Blackburn answered, gazing like Wogan, McCord, Gomez and Edge at the twice-folded piece of paper which came out of the envelope.

14

On the paper was a short, unpunctuated, badly spelled message which took the half-breed only a few seconds to read. He scanned it without expression, against a background of low moans of misery from Travis. Then he turned the letter upside down and placed it on the table so that the seated Blackburn and Wogan, standing beside him, could read it.

"The fellers that gave you the letter told you to bring it to Paraiso, kid?" the half-breed asked.

"Sure, mister. In a hick village down near Mesa del Huracan close to the Sonora-Chihuahua line. Give me the twenty-five bucks and said they'd heard you was stayin' here. If you wasn't, I was to forget it. Unless I wanted to take the trouble to find you and get my hundred bucks."

"Obliged, kid," Edge said, reaching out with both hands to draw in the letter and all the money in the pot except for two fifty-dollar bills.

"You got yourself hurt for no good reason, Travis, you crazy bastard!" Blackburn growled. "The letter's on the level and I figure the game always was, too."

Edge put the letter back in the envelope and the envelope into a shirt pocket. Then he stacked the money, rolled it and pushed it into a hip pocket.

Travis continued to groan as the flow of blood from his sliced eyeballs ceased. McCord looked eager to pick up his money and leave, but seemed nervously reluctant to approach the table yet. Gomez watched with disappointment as Blackburn and Wogan took their cue from Edge and put away their money.

"I never seen nothin' like that before," Blackburn said with admiration in his eyes and voice as Edge got to his feet.

"Me neither, that's for sure," Wogan added, shaking his head slowly. "For a man to carry a razor as a weapon like that. And use it the way you do. It's amazin'."

"Sure is. And cold as ice, too." This from Blackburn as Edge dug the makings from the second pocket in his

15

shirt and began to roll a cigarette. "You're an amazin' man, Edge, or Hedges, or whatever the hell your name is."

"Shit on that, you sonsofbitches!" Travis snarled, and screamed as he pulled his hands away from his face and the blood, congealing fast in the heat, tore at the edges of his wound. "The bastard blinded me!"

"Explains why you can't see things from our point of view!" Blackburn snapped, and cackled with laughter.

"Hedges or Edge," the half-breed growled as he moved toward the door which gave onto the cantina's back rooms. "I'm just an ordinary kind of feller. Object to being accused of something I didn't do, is all."

"Frig you, what about me!" Travis shrieked.

Edge kicked the door fully open. "You, feller? You're outta sight."

The Drummer

*This interlude in the life of Josiah C. Hedges took place
before the War Between the States started; i.e. in terms
of the* Edge *series of books it fits into chronological order ahead of the first-war-flashback title* Killer's Breed.

IT was early evening with the light failing and the heat
of the August day almost exhausted. The two Hedges
boys walked back across the fallow field after fixing the
western boundary fence.

Josiah was the elder of the two by twelve years. A
tall, lean, strong-looking twenty-three-year-old with
clear blue eyes and long black hair, Josiah had to keep
his stride unnaturally short in order that his kid brother
could stay alongside him.

Had Jamie been able-bodied, there would have been
no trouble in matching the pace of his elder brother for
he was tall for his age—only three inches shorter than
the six-foot-three frame of Josiah. But Jamie was lame
in the right leg and, although he could walk without a
stick, it was necessary for him to use both hands to lift
and swing forward his crippled limb at each step.

He was a sandy-haired, fresh-faced, good-looking
youngster, his skin freckled rather than tanned by the
summer sun of central Iowa.

"We done good today, didn't we, Joe?" Jamie said as
they neared the small frame house with the bigger stor-
age barn beside it, the buildings enclosed by a neat
white picket fence.

Beyond the fence to the south was a corral contain-

17

ing six grazing horses. Further south, and to the north and west of the house and barn were fields of ripening wheat. Eastwards, beyond the live oak which grew in the front yard of the house, the prairie extended into seeming infinity with only a wagon-wide trail to mar its otherwise virgin appearance.

"*Did* good, Jamie," the elder brother corrected as he peered out through the gathering dusk along the trail where he thought he had seen something moving. "Or did well would be better."

The youngster grimaced. "A little slip like that don't . . . doesn't mean I have to do more than the hour with the books tonight, does it?"

A dog barked, then came scampering around from the front yard. A small black-and-white mongrel named Patch who did a skidding turn and forced himself between the two brothers for the final few yards to the house.

"Just the usual hour, I guess," Josiah allowed. "But that's even if the company decides to stay."

"Company, Joe?" Jamie looked in the same direction as his brother and spotted the covered wagon that was lumbering in on the trail, still more than a mile distant. He grinned broadly. "Hey, be nice to see some folks, won't it?" He stooped to ruffle the fur between the dog's ears. "Company's coming, Patch."

"Stoke the fire and put some coffee on," Josiah instructed, not sharing the enthusiasm of Jamie and the tail-wagging dog. "Then get washed up."

"Sure, Joe."

While the younger Hedges went into the single-storey house which, moments later, shafted the light of a kerosene lamp through the open doorway and two flanking windows, Josiah crossed the yard to enter the barn where he stored the two hammers, pliers, bag of nails and what was left of the coil of wire after the boundary-fence repairs.

The frown which had settled on his face when he first saw the approaching wagon was still firmly fixed in place when he emerged from the barn. And he directed constant suspicious glances out along the trail as he went toward the house.

He was by nature a cautious young man, never willing to accept anything or anyone at face value. It was a trait of character inherited, like the ice blueness of his eyes, from a Swedish mother. Whereas Jamie, who showed not a single physical clue that there was Latin blood in his veins, was as easy-going and trusting as their Mexican father.

"They close enough yet to recognize?" the excited Jamie asked as he came out of the coffee-smelling kitchen, his face clean and toweling his hands dry.

"Nobody from town has reason to visit us," Josiah answered pensively as he moved into the kitchen to wash up and did no more than glance surreptitiously at the Starr rifle which was lodged on brackets above the fireplace in the spartanly furnished parlor.

"Me and Patch'll go out and be ready to welcome them, Joe."

"You'll stay in the house!" the elder brother ordered from the kitchen. Then took the harshness from his tone. "Set the table, uh? I don't know for how many yet."

As he washed the dirt and sweat from his face, Josiah realized he needed a shave. But there was no time. No time, either, for Jamie and he to change out of their denim dungarees and work-stained boots and check shirts.

When he came out of the kitchen, he could hear the slow clop of hooves and turning wheels on the trail which stretched eight miles from town and dead-ended at the Hedges farmstead. Jamie was standing in the doorway, Patch sitting beside him.

"Strangers, Joe," the boy reported. "Man and a lady. Citified. Selling something, I bet you."

Jamie did not turn around, so was unaware that his brother went to the sideboard, eased open a drawer and took out one of a pair of Colt Little Dragoon revolvers. A gun small enough to slide into a pocket of his dungarees.

"Evenin' to you, son," a man with a raucous voice called as the wagon came to a halt. "Your pa about?"

Josiah showed himself at the doorway, right hand in his pocket and fisted around the butt of the gun.

"Oh, there you are, sir," the newcomer said as he began to climb down from the wagon seat.

He could see the Hedges boys only in silhouette against the kerosene lamp light, for the moon had not yet made much impression on the gloom of dusk. This light shone brightly on the white-painted fence and reached far enough beyond for the unsmiling elder brother to receive a general impression of the wagon driver and the passenger he was helping down to the ground outside the gate.

The man was in his fifties, about two inches under six-foot tall and heavily built, with excess flesh rather than muscular development. He had a round, dark-toned face and wore eyeglasses, the lenses of which sparkled in the fringes of light from the house. His garb was city-style—a pale-colored suit, a vest with a watch chain across the front, a black string tie and derby hat. And his shoes were black and white.

"We're brothers," Josiah corrected as the man ushered the woman toward the gate, ahead of where the two team horses stood quietly in their traces.

"Ah, the Hedges," the man answered with a vigorous nodding of his head as he reached the gate. "May we?"

"Come on in. Coffee pot's on the stove."

"Many thanks, young sir. I'm Jordan Krantz and this here is my daughter, Dawn. We are most pleased to make your acquaintance. Josiah and James, is it not? Unless we were misinformed in your local town."

Dawn was a girl rather than a woman. As tall as her father, but much thinner, with the merest suggestions of feminine curves at her hips and breasts, even though the plain white dress she wore fitted snugly from high neckline to narrow waist. She was seventeen or eighteen at the most, with black hair cut short and dark eyes that were somehow too large for her small, pale face.

As the newcomers came closer to the light source,

20

Josiah saw that Jordan Krantz's face was colored red and blue, similar to that of many of the barflies who frequented the town saloon. Dawn's complexion was marred by red and black spots on her chin and to each side of her nose.

"You got told right, sir," Jamie said. "But I like to be called Jamie."

"That's fine, young feller," Krantz acknowledged, and ignored the younger Hedges. "Say hello to the head of the house, Dawn."

The girl did not quite succeed in holding back a sigh before she greeted Josiah dully with, "It's nice to meet you, sir."

She sounded as weary as they both looked, while her father—after a brief scowl at her lack of enthusiasm—strove to maintain his ebullient mood.

"Krantz is my name and sellin's my game," he announced, hand brushing trail dust from his suit before accepting Josiah's gestured invitation to enter the house. "Pots, pans, eatin' utensils, tools for the house and farm. Hello, little dog. My, you boys have a nice place here. Metal parts for wagon repairs. Oil lamps. Some toys for the younger members of the family. And a special line in the latest patent medicines from the East and even Europe."

"We don't need any of that," Josiah said evenly, as he gestured for the Krantzes to sit down in the two most comfortable chairs which faced each other across the front of the empty fireplace. "Go get coffee for our company, Jamie. Anyway, Mr. Krantz, we always buy what we need from the stores in town."

Dawn sank gratefully into one of the upholstered armchairs while her father moved about the room, touching furniture with the tips of his stubby fingers and glancing through doorways into the kitchen and two bedrooms.

"Then you've probably got some of my lines around, sir," Krantz countered. "Mostly my business is transacted with storekeepers. But when folks live way out in the country like you do, and they're on the route my

21

daughter and I are takin', we like to stop by. Service to them. Convenient. And cheaper. Sellin' direct, you get what you want at the wholesale price."

"Lots of things we want, Mr. Krantz," Josiah said as he sat down at the table. "Nothing we need right now."

Jamie emerged from the kitchen, using his stick now, so that he could carry two tin mugs of steaming, aromatic coffee in his free hand. Patch was at his heels, but the dog chose to sit down close to Dawn after the boy had set the mugs into the hearth.

The girl smiled for the first time, showing crooked teeth. And she thanked the boy and made him blush as she picked up the coffee and sipped at it. The hot drink was obviously as welcome to her as the comfort of the chair.

"You have any objection, sir?" Krantz asked, taking a leather-covered liquor flask from a side pocket of his jacket. "I find coffee unpalatable without a little somethin' extra to flavor it."

"No," Josiah allowed as Jamie returned to the kitchen, still embarrassed by the girl's words and smile. "This house isn't on the route to anywhere."

Krantz brought his mug from the hearth to the table, sat down opposite the elder Hedges and nodded as he poured at least three fingers of rye into the coffee.

"Figured that out soon as I learned you were the Hedges boys. Realized then I must have taken the wrong fork west of town." He shrugged his broad, fleshy shoulders. "But it's an ill wind, like they say. And a travelin' man must try to do business wherever he happens to travel to."

"He's said he don't want nothin', Pa," Dawn put in wearily, as Jamie set down a mug of coffee in front of his brother, hesitated, and went to sit in the chair facing the girl.

The drummer's green eyes, magnified by the lenses of his spectacles, were momentarily clouded by anger at his daughter's words. But he controlled the emotion as he took a swig at the whiskey-laced coffee. Then he gave one of his vigorous nods. And shared a smile between the girl and Josiah.

"Dawn's a fine influence on me, sir. Sometimes I get too wrapped up in my work and the products I sell. Talk too much to listen to what other folks are sayin'. Already I've seen you and your brother are runnin' a fine place and have just about everythin' I sell."

His smile seemed to Josiah to be as forced and false as everything else about the man's attitude. Which perhaps was an indication that much of what he had said lacked truth. Certainly the west fork outside of town, which the Krantz wagon would have reached in full daylight, was clearly signposted. And the drummer had reached the Hedges farmstead armed at least with the names of the man and boy who ran the place situated at the dead end of an eight-mile trail across otherwise unsettled prairie.

What other information about the Hedges had Krantz picked up in town? Perhaps a particular detail which had encouraged him to come.

"Yes, sir, a really fine place," the drummer went on. "Heard in town how you boys took over after your poor ma and pa died. It seems folks have a lot of admiration for you and young James . . . Jamie."

"You'll stay for supper?" Josiah asked, his suspicion of the man's motives becoming mixed with irritation at the condescending tenor of his talk. "It's just cold cuts and salad."

"We don't like to impose, Mr. Hedges," Dawn said, and Josiah saw his brother's face cloud with disappointment. Then brighten again when the girl's father countered:

"You are as highly thought of by your neighbors for your hospitality as for your hard work, sir. Dawn is correct. We have no wish to trouble you, but if you insist, we will be most happy and grateful to join you in your evenin' meal. And since there is now a female in your house, at least you will be relieved of the chores of preparin' supper. If young Jamie will show my daughter where things are kept?"

23

Josiah did not protest and the boy, obviously moon-struck by the girl, went eagerly with her into the kitchen. Patch went with them and stayed close by Dawn through every move she made in setting out the table for four people and then preparing and serving the meal. During this process and then over the meal itself and while Dawn and Jamie cleared and washed the dirty dishes, Jordan Krantz talked constantly.

About himself and his daughter, his dead wife, his travels from his native New Orleans and of the wide variety of jobs he held before he became a hardware salesman. Throughout this monologue, Jamie kept glancing at Dawn and blushing when she saw him and smiled. The girl was for the most part wearily bored, and Josiah did his best to conceal the nagging doubt he felt about Krantz's presence at the house.

"How about a little cards, sir?" the drummer announced as he lit a cheroot and Josiah fired a cigarette, and water began to run on dirty dishes in the kitchen.

"No, Pa!" Dawn shouted anxiously.

"Remember what Ma used to say!" Jamie called, even more concerned than the girl.

The elder brother remembered a great deal of what his mother had told him, which was why he had offered hospitality to the Krantz father and daughter—not trusting the drummer and yet having no specific reason to feel the way he did.

As for Jamie's stridently voiced objection . . .

Jose Aviles had been a gambling man long ago and was only partially reformed by the love of Ingrid Ohlson. Before they married, the beautiful Swedish woman succeeded in persuading Jose that he should not take so many risks, whether at a gaming table or in his attitude to life in general. She succeeded to such an extent that gambling friends of Jose began to call him "Bet-Hedging Aviles." Which suggested to the mixed nationality couple a suitable American name under which they could marry and raise their children in their new country of which they were so proud to be a part.

Jose Hedges never gambled for money after the birth

24

of his first son. But often, as Josiah and later Jamie grew up, he played cards with the boys. With the reluctant approval of his wife who acknowledged that a friendly card game was a pleasant enough way to pass a long winter evening when the prairie norther was lashing rain at the isolated Iowa farmstead.

"Oh, come now, just a friendly game to while away the time while the excellent supper slips down," Krantz said, causing Josiah to start. "If there is any criticism of you at all in town it is that you work too hard and too long. Take too little time off for your amusements."

"Please don't, Joe," Jamie whined.

Had the boy not said this, in the tone he used, his brother might well have declined Krantz's invitation. But the irritation Josiah had earlier felt toward the drummer was briefly directed at Jamie.

"Finish the dishes and then get to your books!" he snapped, using his authority as a man to expunge his resentment toward a mere boy who was seeking to influence him.

Krantz grinned and nodded as he took a deck of cards from an inside pocket of his suit jacket. And leaned forward to whisper: "Our younger kin mean well, sir. But one day they'll be old enough to appreciate a few mild vices of their own. Five-card stud, jacks or higher to open suit you?"

Josiah nodded and experienced a surge of excitement as Krantz shuffled the deck, gave them across the table to be cut and then dealt them. Not since he had played for matchsticks with his father had he felt this. And when, after dealing two cards face down and one face up, Krantz dug a handful of loose change from his pocket, the fire of anticipation burned fiercely in the younger man's belly.

He continued to be his mother's son by distrusting the drummer. But knew he was most definitely his father's offspring in the way his long dormant penchant for gambling was reawakened.

"You'll have to wait a while, Mr. Krantz," he said, and rose from the table to go into Jamie's bedroom.

25

There, in the angle of the north and west walls, he dropped to his haunches and pried up a floorboard. Beneath was a box containing every cent which he and his brother possessed. Ninety-five dollars, mostly in bills but a few dollars in coins. First he took just the dimes, nickels and cents. Then, with a grimace of guilt, he withdrew ten one-dollar bills.

While he was in the bedroom, he heard the Krantzes talking, and a door close. On returning to the parlor he saw that Jamie was hunched in an armchair, head hung over an open book. The boy made an obvious point of not looking up at his elder brother.

Krantz capped his flask and said, "Hope you don't mind, sir. I've asked Dawn to see that the horses are watered."

Josiah merely nodded as he took his seat at the table and let the handful of change drop to the top. Although he tried to tell himself the resentment he felt was directed toward Jamie, he knew it was in vain. Rather, the drummer and a weakness in his own character combined to attack his peace of mind.

They played several quiet hands, betting and raising in pennies. Then Jamie, making no secret of his lack of concentration on the English primer, slapped the book closed.

"I'll go see how Miss Dawn is doing," he said.

"An hour," Josiah reminded firmly. "Take it into your room if it'll be better."

Jamie looked petulantly at Josiah, but saw from the way his brother's eyes narrowed to glinting slits that it would serve no purpose to argue or even plead. Then, as he always did on the infrequent occasions when there was friction between them, the boy over-emphasized his limp. He made to slam his bedroom door, but caught another glimpse of the hard, cold, ice-blue eyes. And shut himself in his room quietly.

"Damn shame about the accident that crippled the boy," Krantz said with a shake of his head.

Josiah curled back his thin lips from his teeth. "Anything the folks in town didn't tell you about us, mister?" he growled.

The scowl and rasping tone brought a deeper frown to the drummer's face. "Sorry, sir, I can understand why you don't like the matter raised."

Still not his usual calm self, Josiah looked at his hole cards, took a dollar bill from his dungarees pocket and pushed it into the center of the table.

"Ah," Krantz said, and dug into a pocket of his own to cover the bet.

There was no further talk until the younger man won a ten-dollar pot. Then he said, as Dawn re-entered the house, "Just so you know the true story, Mr. Krantz. I was just a kid myself when it happened. We were playing around with that rifle you see hanging over the mantelshelf. It shouldn't have been loaded, but it was. It fired and Jamie'll have a lame leg for the rest of his life."

Krantz nodded mournfully as the cards were dealt. "There is tragedy in the life of everyone, sir. Why, when my dear wife died soon after givin' birth to Dawn there—"

"Forget it, Pa," the girl said from the chair to the right of the hearth, Patch squatting beside her again. "Finish your game and let's get movin'. The horses are all watered and rested well enough now."

Josiah was not so intently interested in his cards that he failed to see the frown of puzzlement which the father directed toward the daughter.

The betting was all in dollars now and in less than an hour, as Dawn stared directly ahead and absently ruffled Patch's fur, Josiah took more than fifty off Krantz, who won occasionally but never so much as he had lost in the previous hand.

Then, with twenty-seven dollars in a pot and Jordan Krantz needing six to call upon Josiah Hedges to show, the drummer took a crumpled bill from his pocket and gazed at it with miserable surprise.

"I could have sworn it was a five spot," he groaned.

In those games long ago with his father, Josiah had

27

learned more than the mere techniques of playing cards, and living life. One such tenet which had been impressed upon him—out of earshot of his mother— was that, unless the circumstances were special, a man should neither give nor ask any quarter.

"Means you're going to have to fold then?"

"I guess so . . . unless . . . ?"

"We don't need anything off your wagon, Mr. Krantz."

The fires of anger burned briefly in the green eyes behind the spectacle lenses. And there was a note of irritation in the drummer's tone when he retorted, "You've already made that plain." Then he moderated his voice as he nodded toward his daughter. "I have somethin' else to trade, Mr. Hedges. Earlier you asked if there was anythin' about you your neighbors did not tell me. I don't know. But certainly there is much talk about the lack of a female out here. Seems quite a few of the local girls would like to set their caps at you, given half a chance."

Josiah's face was impassive as he shifted his gaze from the father to the daughter. She showed that, although her thoughts might have been on matters beyond the room, she was aware of what was being said at the table. She turned her head and her dark eyes met the blue ones of the young man and held his gaze, responding to it with the same lack of expression.

"You understand what Pa is sayin', Mr. Hedges? It's happened before when he gets into a tight money spot, so you won't be spoilin' nothin' for me. Win or lose the hand, you get the best I can give. And there ain't never been no comlpaints."

"That there hasn't, sir," Krantz augmented, enthusiastic in stark contrast to the girl's even tempered resignation.

Josiah pursed his lips and, still looking at Dawn, said, "Tell you what I'd like, Mr. Krantz."

"Name it, sir."

The inherited traits and the teachings of both his parents came together now, as he shifted his gaze from the

28

girl to the man and looked at him with an expression of depthless malevolence. The words he spoke were as frigid as the glint in his eyes.

"Like for you to get up from this table, take your daughter outside, climb aboard your wagon and roll it away from this farm."

Krantz had straightened on his chair as if from some palpable power emanated by the younger man's expression, and seemed to come more erect with each word directed at him.

He licked his lips before he countered, "An honorable man would give another the opportunity to get even, sir!"

"I don't see another honorable man here," came the response. "Do like I told you."

"And if I refuse?"

Josiah hooked his palms over the rim of the table and began to push himself to his feet. "Then I'll have to throw you out, mister."

"Stay where you are, Joe!"

He froze his frame in a half upright attitude and turned his head to look at Dawn. There was a small revolver in her right hand, one side of her dress hem still rucked up after she had drawn the gun from a holster strapped to her calf. She remained in the chair with only her expression changed. She was at once sad and anxious.

"I'm truly sorry, Joe," she said less shrilly. "You and your kid brother don't deserve to have callers like us."

"He's already said he doesn't need anythin' from us, girl!" her father snarled, pushing back his chair and getting to his feet. "That includes sympathy. The boy's bedroom is where he got the money from. Go get the rest of it."

Krantz had drawn a gun now. A small Sharps four-barrel derringer which he aimed at Josiah with his left hand while he scooped up all the paper money from the table with his right. Most of it was his own.

"This is nothin' to what you have hid away in there, is it?" he rasped with an evil grin of triumph. "Hard workin' young man like you who doesn't live in the lap of luxury and won't even spring the price of a church social ticket for a local girl. You're a fool, you know that, Mr. Josiah Hedges? You could have been beddin' my daughter while I got your pile. That offer was on the level. Reckon it would have made the loss a little easier to take. Well, girl? Go get the money!"

Dawn had put her gun away, headed for the door to Jamie's room, then halted.

Patch, who had never been more than a pet and rodent catcher around the farm, continued to sit by her vacated chair, head on one side and ears pricked.

"What about the boy, Pa?"

"He's a kid and a cripple! He's not about to give you any trouble!"

"Like hell I ain't!"

The retort was roared by Jamie as he flung open the door of his room and hurled himself across the threshold. It was obvious he had been listening at the door and his timing was perfect. A match for his positioning. His flying tackle caught the girl completely off guard. The top of his head cracked hard into the side of her thigh and his arms encircled her below the knees.

She screamed in shock, then cried out in pain as she was sent to the floor, Jamie's arms still fastened securely around her legs.

With amazement and then rage deepening the unhealthy color of his face, Jordan Krantz snapped his head around to look toward the mêlée in the doorway.

He was distracted for just part of a second. But this was long enough for Josiah, who did not have to turn his head to see his brother's spectacular entry into the parlor. His hands were still hooked over the rim of the table and he had not moved from the stance into which the girl's gun had frozen him. Thus, he was ideally poised to jerk erect, this action adding power to the action of lifting and pushing the table.

Perhaps Jordan Krantz intended to fire a shot from his gun. Or maybe the twitch of his trigger finger was just a part of his nervous reaction as he swung his head and saw the heavy table tilting toward him. Whichever, he had no chance of hitting Josiah Hedges,. who was already crouching in the cover of the overturning table, struggling to get the Little Dragoon out of his capacious pocket.

The report of the small .22 bullet leaving one of the four barrels was almost drowned by the excited barking of Patch as the dog lunged forward and began to skip around the struggling forms of Jamie and Dawn, tail wagging and tongue lolling out.

Krantz vented a bellow of pain as he fell backward over his chair, which was abruptly curtailed as the top of his head cracked against the floor. And thus he felt no more pain as the table, totally overturned, thudded into his knees which were folded across the toppled chair.

"Pa!" Dawn shrieked, as she ceased to struggle against Jamie and stared with horror on her face across the floor to where her father was sprawled out on his back. "He's bleedin'!"

Josiah came erect and moved around the disarrayed furniture to look down at the unconscious drummer.

It was not the exploded bullet which had harmed Krantz but the gun which had fired it. As he reeled back from the toppling table, the man had raised both hands to protect his florid face. Either he had brought his gun hand up too forcefully, or the impact of his skull against the floor had provided the necessary power. Whichever, the metal of barrels and hammer had shattered the lenses of his spectacles. And his eyelids and upper cheeks were sheened with blood which oozed from around the countless tiny shards of embedded glass.

"He'll live, miss," the elder Hedges announced levelly after watching the strong rise and fall of the broad chest for a few moments. "There's a gun under the skirts of her dress, Jamie. Girl like her won't have any call to complain if you look for it. Then let her up."

"Oh, what a mess," Dawn groaned as she submitted to having the boy raise her dress and draw the revolver from the holster.

Then she watched in horrified fascination as the elder brother searched among the money scattered on the floor for a particular crumpled bill, which he pushed into the top pocket of her father's suit jacket.

"I didn't win that one," Josiah explained evenly.

"What . . . what are you gonna do with us?" she asked as she got shakily to her feet. "Pa's got glass in his face. He needs a doctor."

"You came from town. So you know the way back there. Doc Patterson will take care of him."

"But how—?"

He pushed the small Colt back into his pocket, lifted the table off Krantz's legs and then, with an easy strength, stooped and raised the much bigger man up and over his shoulder. The glassless spectacles dropped to the floor.

Patch, disconsolate the game was over, ambled across, sniffed the frames, then went into the kitchen and began to lap water.

"Bring both guns outside, Jamie," Josiah instructed and nodded toward the door. "After you, miss."

She was on the point of asking for something, but received no encouragement from the face of the elder Hedges. And so silently did what he indicated.

Outside, in the pleasantly warm, brightly moonlit night, Josiah had to use every ounce of his strength to hoist the big, unconscious man up onto the wagon seat.

"I really did mean it, Joe," the girl blurted suddenly. "Most times I go along with Pa's cheatin' ways. But honestly, when I saw the way you and Jamie are, how fine things are here, the way you treated us so well . . . I—"

"Sure, Miss Krantz," Josiah interrupted after he had climbed down from the wagon. He took the two guns from Jamie, who looked almost as miserable as the girl, and tossed them through the front flap of the covered wagon. They clanged against the hardware stowed in the back and the sound roused Jordan Krantz to the first stage of recovering consciousness.

Then he went to stand in the gateway. Slowly, as the girl climbed wearily up on to the wagon seat, Jamie came to stand beside him. Then Patch emerged from the house, stopped to wet at the base of the live oak, and ran forward to sit between the brothers.

The sounds of the drummer's awakening were covered by the clop of hooves, creak of timbers and rumble of wheelrims as Dawn turned the wagon around.

"Ma always said no good ever came from gambling, Joe," Jamie muttered. "And I sure enough reckon Miss Dawn could be a nice lady if her pa wasn't such a—"

"Reckon we're the best part of eighty dollars to the good, young feller," his brother cut in brightly, eager to cheer up the boy.

"Dawn!" Jordan Krantz cried, shrill with terror. "Where are you Dawn? I can't see you daughter!"

"I'm here, Pa!" the girl shouted above his hysteria. "Right here with you, Pa."

"Joe, he might be blinded for life," Jamie gasped, deeply concerned.

"Something else Ma used to say," Josiah Hedges responded.

"Uh?"

"Always darkest before Dawn."

Chapter Two

THERE was a clearly defined marker at the side of the trail to show where New Mexico ended and old Mexico began. Whether it was in precisely the right territorial position—on the line agreed by the government of two countries—was not important. The pinnacle of rock with a splash of black paint at the base was accepted in good faith by all who passed it, and all who stopped at it to turn back, as proof they had reached the international boundary.

Three times a year, a man who had no official capacity, rode south from Paraiso with a pot of paint to throw at the base of the rock so that the sign was always easy to see.

The man called Edge rode past the marker at noon astride a well-rested gray mare, and the man himself looked in good shape, too. This not just because he had spent two weeks resting up in Paraiso's Oro Blanco Cantina after surviving the events which took place in a town called San Lucas built on a rise known as *El Cerro de Muerto*. For, prior to leaving the cantina, he had taken the time to soak in a bathtub and to shave, and he had not yet been in the saddle long enough for the passing of time, the furnace heat of the sun or the gray dust of the trail to make many inroads on his fresh cleanliness.

As he rode beyond the marker, he took the makings from a shirt pocket, rolled a cigarette, hung it at a corner of his wide mouth and lit it. He banished from his mind all thoughts of the long-ago past, which had been triggered by the contents of the letter rather than the fact of a card game leading to a man being blinded. For Travis, with or without pain and misery, meant nothing to him, whereas Jamie had meant a great deal. So had the farm, and his whole life before the start of the war.

Yet the short letter delivered by McCord referred to an event which had taken place in the much more recent past . . .

He shook his head, almost imperceptibly, and scowled briefly. Later, if the writer of the letter was truthful, it would be necessary to reflect on that aspect of what had gone by. Now, riding south on this Mexican stretch of an outlaw trail, it was imperative to concentrate his entire attention on the present and the potential dangers it might hold.

So, as he rode the mare on a light rein at an easy walking pace, he constantly shifted his eyes back and forth along their narrow sockets, every now and then glancing back over his shoulder, and listening intently for any sound that might signal hidden trouble.

Yet he rode in an apparently casual attitude, his lean face expressionless and his frame revealing no clue to the fact that he was poised to respond in just part of a second if his freedom or survival should be threatened.

He was dressed in a gray cotton shirt, black denim pants, black riding boots without spurs, gray kerchief knotted loosely at the throat and wide-brimmed, low-crowned Stetson which shaded his face. Since his shave in the cantina at Paraiso, the suggestion of a moustache along his top lip and curving low down to either side of his mouth was more pronounced. Around his waist was a scuffed leather gunbelt with a bullet slotted into every loop. The holster which hung from the right, tied down to his thigh, carried a virtually brand-new Army Colt revolver. The Winchester rifle, its stock jutting from the boot slung from the forward right of the saddle, was a great deal older. The saddle itself was of the Western kind favored by cowpunchers, hung with two well-stocked bags and a pair of filled canteens. Lashed on behind was a bedroll with a knee-length black leather coat tied on top.

Thus was Edge as well supplied as any man could be for a long ride through the barren, hostile, relentlessly cruel Sierra Madre country. A ride under the blistering sun which, as it sank behind the distant, jagged ridges would herald a cold and dangerous night for a man to rest.

As well supplied as any man could be . . . but more experienced than most in dealing with the rigors of such a ride. For cruelly few of the trails Edge had followed since he left the Iowa farmstead after the end of the war—with the mutilated body of Jamie buried beneath the live oak in the front yard—had been safe and easy.

He maintained the same easy pace and the same degree of vigilance for the greater part of the afternoon, staying on the hoof-pounded trail as it swung to left and right, taking the line of least resistance but constantly on an up-grade. Passing along arroyos, cutting through gullies, following the bases of escarpments and swinging around mesas. Beneath the vivid blueness of the cloudless sky the landscape was mostly colored gray by rock and dust. But here and there was an outcrop of red sandstone, and, less frequently, patches of tough green grass, brown brush and clumps of cacti and stunted trees.

Edge placed the time at about four o'clock when he reined the mare to a halt at a point where the trail reached the crest of a shallow slope and curved southwest into the mouth of what appeared to be a low-sided canyon. The western wall of the canyon mouth offered some shade in which the temperature was a few degrees lower than in the direct glare of the sun and some dusty grass sprouted up among the scattered rocks at the base of the cliff. When he had dismounted and while he took a mouthful of water from a canteen, the horse sidled away to check out the grass and then began to crop at it with an obvious lack of enthusiasm.

The half-breed hooked the canteen back over the saddlehorn and then squatted down on a smoothtoped boulder and leaned his back against the rock wall. He raised a hand to touch the shirt pocket in which the letter was stowed, but did not take out the envelope. Instead, he delved into the other pocket to take out the makings. While he smoked the cigarette, he kept watch over his back trail for as far as he could see it.

Travis was in no condition to seek revenge and it would take him a long time to raise the money to pay others to do the job. But Blackburn and Wogan? They had been riding south to reach Paraiso. Outlaws, bounty hunters or simply drifters? Unknown to each other until they met up in town. But they had been drinking together when Edge left the Oro Blanco Cantina, spending some of the small money they won in the poker game, and maybe eager for a bigger stake. Either individually or as a result of joint planning, they might consider it worthwhile to track the biggest winner, backshoot him and—

A rifle shot cracked. And a horse snorted in pain against the reverberating series of echoes from the report.

Edge powered to his feet, right hand dropping to and fisting around the butt of the holstered Colt. As his head snapped to the side, his eyes shifted from the empty terrain to the north and fixed on the deserted entrance to the canyon.

The mare had moved from sight between the thirty-feet-high rock walls, obviously tempted to search for lusher grass. Although unseen, the horse could be heard. There was a heavy thud as the animal crashed to the ground, followed by a more subdued snort, then a snicker and finally a venting of the last breath forced out between quivering lips.

Men shouted in unison with the sounds made by the dying mare, speaking Spanish from many yards beyond where the animal died.

"You idiot, Ramon! You have killed only a horse!" This man enraged.

"I did not know this, Pedro! I see something move

and I fire! By instinct!" Ramon sounded frightened.

"That looks like a fine horse, too!" Regretful.

There was a chorus of exclamations that expressed agreement with this. "Be quiet, you sons of whores!" Pedro snarled and had the authority to ensure that the order was obeyed. "A fine horse with a saddle on the back does not run free and wild in the Sierra Madre!"

More exclamations of agreement, less strident this time and quickly fading into silence, as the Mexicans mused on the whereabouts of the rider of the dead horse and awaited an order from their leader.

Edge, his lean, deeply lined face impassive again after a momentary scowl at this new twist of harsh fate, had begun to move as soon as he heard that there were more than two men beyond the canyon mouth. Five or six at least, he guessed. Too many and too distant to be handled with just an Army Colt and the straight razor.

So he turned away from the gap between the rock faces and broke into a loping run when he was certain the intervening high ground would act as a barrier to the sounds he made. Dust rose from under his pumping feet and clung to the sweat which the exertion oozed from the pores on his face. The grade was downwards for a while, then across the slope and finally upwards, the increasing steepness forcing the half-breed to slow his pace. He was about four hundred yards west of the gap in the rock faces by then, unable to hear anything except his own labored breathing.

To reach his initial objective he had to locate hand- and foot-holds on an almost sheer climb of fifteen feet. And because there was no opportunity to brush them away, beads of salt sweat trickled into his eyes and made them sting. The hat fell off his head, but was held to his back by the neck thong. He realized the long dead cigarette stub was still adhered to his lower lip and he spat it out.

At the top of the climb, squatting on his haunches and sucking in the arid Mexican air, he took the time to rub the sweat from his eyes and peer northward. From this higher vantage point he could see further out along

38

the trail. Neither Blackburn nor Wogan nor anything else was moving this side of the shimmering heat haze that foreshortened the horizon.

Then he looked in the other directions. Two buzzards were circling at the top of a high thermal far to the south. There were no other signs that anything except rugged plant life existed in the area of the Sierra Madre that came within his range of vision.

The ground sloped gently away from him in a series of long curving steps back toward what he thought had been a canyon. And rose in a similar geographical formation on the other side, but not a canyon, though. Instead, a convoluted valley snaking in broad sweeps toward the south-west entered from the north via a narrow, fifty-yard-long natural cutting.

There was plenty of cover in the valley, from timber, hollows and boulders which featured the slopes to either side of the trail. So he approached the rim of the cutting cautiously, aware that one or more of the Mexicans could have been posted to watch for a man who skylined himself on the high ground while the others advanced on the spot where the dead horse lay.

Then he achieved cover himself, on his side of the thirty-foot-wide cutting. For, spread back from and along the rim, was a liberal scattering of boulders similar to those at the base among which the mare had originally begun to crop.

Long ago—probably millions of years in the prehistoric past—this area of the Sierra Madre had been much higher. But there had been a geological fault through the rock strata which had eventually submitted to a build-up of enormous pressures. The seemingly immovable rock had split in two and the highest pinnacles had crumbled. Some great fragments had crashed down into the newly opened chasm. Other pieces remained on the rim and back from it. And it was these which Edge crawled among, sometimes having to pass over cracks of up to a foot wide, as he neared the rim.

"Hey, Pedro, I do not see anybody," Ramon reported. "Maybe the gringo was shot or just died, and the horse, he has been wandering loose."

"She, idiot. It was a mare," the leader of the group growled.

"I did not notice."

"If you had the sense to see what is before your eyes, we would have had one fine horse, Ramon!"

Edge heard the exchange, and the scornful sounds which followed it before he was in a position to risk a glance down into the cutting.

"It is done and cannot be undone. Jesus, see what we have except for the saddle and bedroll. Ramon, keep watch to the north. Boy, you guard us from the south."

Edge peered down into the cutting for no more than a second, his glinting, almost closed eyes recording all there was to be seen.

Five men, mostly hidden from above by their large sombreros since they were all close to the base of the cliff, gathered around the carcass of the dead mare. In compliance with the orders of the leader, Ramon ambled away to the left, to take up a sentry position at the mouth of the cutting; another member of the group moved faster in the other direction; a third stopped to check over the saddle and other accoutrements on the horse. While the leader watched this man, his arms akimbo, the fifth Mexican maintained a hold on the reins of a scrawny-looking, ill-equipped horse. All of them carried a rifle and as the two sentries moved to left and right, the half-breed was able to see they wore gunbelts with holsters and crossed bandoliers.

This seen, Edge withdrew his head from the rim, knowing from his own highly developed sixth sense for such things that a man did not actually have to see a watcher to realize he was being watched. He rolled onto his back and pushed his hat forward to shade his eyes from the sun which was more than halfway down the western dome of the sky, listening to the talk below him, allowing time and events to decide his course of action.

"It is a good saddle, Pedro," Jesus reported. "Better

40

than the one you have. The Winchester is no better no worse than those we have. Fine blankets. One canteen, it is full. The other almost full. The food in the bags, it is not touched. The horse has not been ridden far."

"I do not like it," Pedro growled.

"That Ramon killed the fine horse?"

Pedro spat noisily. "That the rider of the horse has not been seen. A fresh horse. Plenty of food and water. From Paraiso it must have come. The man who rode her could well have been killed between there and here. By a very rich killer to allow such a fine horse and all that is upon her to escape."

"So what are we going to do about it, Pedro," a new voice asked.

Edge placed him as the one holding the live horse. And the half-breed waited calmly for the response, lips pursed and eyes open and gazing up into the sweaty darkness of the underside of his hat.

"We are five and he, if he is around here, is but one," the leader answered after a pause for several seconds. "I think this is a good place to wait for the *Federale* bastards. From where the boy is the whole north end of the valley can be seen. And from Ramon's position our rear can be guarded. When the *Federales* come—or should any gringo ride through from the border—this is the perfect place for the ambush, I think."

Edge curled back his lips so that the sinking sun glinted on his teeth. It would not be necessary, at least in the immediate future, to take a long chance on blasting difficult downward shots with a low velocity revolver in the faint hope of killing the five rifle-toting Mexicans.

But all he had been allowed was time. Now he had to await events which might or might not present the opportunity to launch a less risky plan.

"There is something I do not like, Pedro."

"What is that, Juan?"

"That we are down here and the man who rode this horse might be up there."

The grin froze on Edge's half-concealed features.

41

"How much do you not like this, Juan?"

"Pardon, Pedro?"

"We have come far today. I have been riding. You and the others were on foot. If you wish for more exercise, you may climb to the high ground. But it would be easier, I think, if you lay down on your back." His faintly taunting tone became suddenly harsh. "And keep your eyes open, Juan! Like Ramon and the boy, you will be on guard!"

Other orders were issued and there were the sounds of them being obeyed, as the scrawny living horse was hobbled and, like the dead one, had the saddle and bedroll removed. Then there was almost complete silence, broken only by the occasional sigh, spit, cough and the scrape of boot leather against the ground.

Edge pushed the Stetson onto the top of his head and rolled over onto his belly. In a higher position than the guards posted at each end of the cutting, he had a better and longer view of the terrain over which the expected *Federales* or a chance rider from Paraiso would approach. Both stretches of country were equally deserted and even the buzzards had gone from the southern sky now. He shortened the focus of his slitted eyes and began to ponder the germ of an idea. He rolled over onto his back again and eased up into a sitting position, shoulders resting against the sun-warmed surface of one of the larger rocks. Seated thus, not moving a muscle, he was able to keep watch over both lengths of trail and would look, to anyone far to the north or south, like just a part of the rock. And he could hear any sound louder than a snore which came from the Mexicans down in the cutting.

For the first hour the vigil became progressively more uncomfortable for he was exposed to the full glare of the sun. Even though he did not move, sweat oozed and trickled. He began to itch in several places. Desert flies settled from time to time on his flesh and crawled over it. His bladder felt filled to bursting point. Time seemed to slow down. He sensed that he could feel the bristles growing on his face.

Then the leading arc of the sun touched the rugged western horizon and shaded from brilliant yellow toward a restful red. And the air cooled as the shadows reached the full extent of their length, none of them moving.

Down in the cutting two men slept while three watched.

The sun went to its daily red death and the twilight was only short-lived before full night clamped down over the Sierra Madre. The pale moon brightened and the star pattern appeared.

"Hey, Jesus, I think you should let me sleep for a while," Juan growled, after Jesus had grunted and cursed, apparently on being shaken awake by Juan.

In the moonlit darkness, the sounds of movement and voices seemed to have a sharper note.

"Pedro said nothing of this," Jesus complained.

"I say something now," the leader of the group put in levelly, with no sleepiness in his voice. "Jesus will take over from Ramon and I will relieve the boy. Those not on guard will sleep."

"But the rider of the horse, Pedro?" Juan pointed out anxiously.

"If he was here and able to move against us, he would have done so. Maybe he was here, I do not know. Already I have said, one man against five. With just a pistol, if anything. For we have his rifle. If you were he in such a position and saw us, Juan?"

"All right, Pedro," Juan allowed doubtfully after a pause.

The leader and Jesus moved away in opposite directions. Edge was able to hear the sounds of voices, but not the words spoken, by the former sentries and the new ones. When Ramon and the boy joined Juan at the base of the cliff face below where the half-breed sat, the worried Mexican tried to interest them in his doubts. He received no response from the boy.

Ramon growled, "You want to watch for him, you watch, my friend. I sleep. To be fresh and ready when the bastard *Federales* come."

43

He spat and sighed.

"I will watch," Juan said softly but forcefully.

"Without talking, uh?" Ramon muttered, and sighed again.

Edge checked the moonlit trail to north and south again, then moved carefully, aware that the crack of a joint, brought into use after a long period of rest, would sound like a gunshot to the ears of the tense Juan.

He began to stack rocks.

It was a time-consuming, nerve-wracking, muscle-straining chore, which he carried out on hands and knees. His normally impassive features were transformed by an expression of teeth-gritted tension each time he carefully lowered a fresh rock onto the growing pile.

He selected the fragments carefully, choosing those with at least two flat sides and weighing between about three and five pounds, building them into a double-thickness dry stone wall, three feet high and two feet in front of the top of the cliff. About six feet long.

The position of the wall was directly above where, from the sounds of their voices and now their snoring, he knew Ramon, the boy and Juan to be. At least twenty feet to the right of where the scrawny horse was hobbled.

It didn't look to be much of a horse, but events had made it the only one available to him, so they had motivated his patient wait and the delicate building operation which engaged him now, the exertion and tension opening his pores wider than the blazing sun ever had.

He knew his plan fell far short of being foolproof. Just a few weeks previously a lone Apache brave had been killed by a single rock hurled down at him. But this was different.

At best, the rocks when he toppled the completed wall would kill the three men immediately under them. And bring Pedro and Jesus running back into the cutting, assuming the fall was the result of some kind of earth tremor. This would give Edge the element of surprise to blast revolver shots at the surviving Mexicans.

But there was a chance that one or more of the men below would evade the rockfall and arrive at the immediate conclusion that Juan's doubts were well founded.

"Hey, the batards are coming!"

Edge froze in the act of lowering another piece of rock on the wall, which as yet was only two feet high and four feet long.

He didn't know how long it had taken to reach this stage and now formed his lips into the shape of an unbroken curse, angry at himself that he had concentrated upon the chore to the exclusion of all else.

As he heard the gleeful voice of Pedro and then the man's running footfalls, his iceblue eyes flickered across their narrow sockets below the hooded lids. He saw the bunch of riders as a slow-moving dark patch against the moonlight-whitened terrain some three miles to the north.

"Wake up, you lazy sonsofwhores!" Pedro snarled. "Jesus, come back here! We have some *Federales* to kill!"

The shape of the snarling curse changed into the line of a brutal grin on the half-breed's lips. The sweating tension of stacking the rocks had been for nothing. But that was of no consequence. It had never been a good plan, simply the only one available which gave him a slender chance of getting Pedro's horse. Much better to let the *Federales* slaughter their fellow countrymen with a little help from Edge which might go beyond warning the soldiers of the ambush.

He set the stone down on the center of the half-finished wall.

The ground trembled, sending a quiver up through his body from his angled knees and bent-over toes.

"What was that?" Juan gasped against the sound of Jesus's running feet hitting the ground.

"What was what, you crazy—?" Pedro started.

But if he had time to complete what he was saying, the words were lost behind a sharp crack of splitting rock. Followed by a low rumbling sound which grew louder with each part of the second that passed.

45

Edge threw himself up onto his haunches as the previously solid and inert ground beneath him tremored and groaned. He had been kneeling on a hairline crack in the rock. Suddenly this opened into an inch-wide fissure. Then yawned wider still, the ground beyond tilting.

The shrillness of the Mexicans' voices sounded above the awesome creaks of rock masses moving under enormous pressures.

In back of where the half-breed powered to his full height and whirled, other cracks opened up or widened.

For countless millions of years, the rim of the cutting into the valley had been finely balanced, the cracks along its top not deep enough to cause a further collapse while the debris of the first fall remained undisturbed.

But Edge had altered the weight distribution. The final stone added to the carefully constructed wall tipped the delicate balance and placed him in as great a danger as the shrieking and screaming Mexicans he was trying to kill.

As the heap of stones fell to the canting rim, then showered downwards with the breaking-up rim itself, he had to leap for his life. Launching himself off one area of trembling rock, across fissures gaping wider by the moment, onto another piece of ground as unstable as that he had left.

The noise of the collapsing cliff was deafening and the billowing cloud of rock dust threatened to engulf and blind him as he leapt and turned, pausing for split seconds to choose the direction for his next move.

Then the sharp sounds of rock splitting ended. And there was just the rumbling and slithering of shattered fragments of rock rolling and sliding down the no-longer-sheer side of the cutting.

Edge lunged onto a downslope and pitched forward, jarred from head to foot by the impact of his fall. For long moments he thought the ground beneath him was still moving, but then realized it was his own body which was shaking.

46

He did not attempt to move until his jarred nervous system quietened and the final falling rock came to a halt. In the utter stillness, a million dust motes settled onto his sprawled, face-down form.

"Sonofabitch," he growled through teeth exposed in a grin as he rolled over onto his back, "They just have to be all stone dead."

The words sounded clearly to his ears as the numbing effect of the rock fall was overcome.

He could not yet hear the hoofbeats of the *Federales'* mounts. As he got to his feet his bruised, painful flesh complained, and he groaned in response.

The dust cloud was thinning enough for him to see that the rock had ceased to crumble less than three feet in back of where he fell. Beyond this point the sheer cliff had been transformed into a one-in-one slope, easy enough to climb down by using the again-inert rocks as uneven steps.

More dust settled on his clothing and adhered to his sweat-tacky face as he picked his way to the bottom of the new slope and all of it was laid by the time he stepped off the rocks. During the descent, he kept a hand draped over the butt of the holstered Colt but did not draw it. The stillness, which had previously been disturbed only by his footfalls, was now invaded by the thud of hooves as the *Federales* rode within earshot, galloping their mounts.

At first glance, the elderly and undernourished gelding of Pedro seemed to be the only living thing to have survived in the cutting. It had managed, although hobbled, to move out from under the shower of rocks which half buried the decomposing carcass of the dead mare.

Edge spoke softly and stroked the neck of the still-terrified animal as he raked his eyes over the cutting which was now three-quarters filled with shattered rocks. The gelding became calm and there were no signs or sounds of life from under the landslide.

The *Federales* rode closer, the cadence of the hoofbeats slowing.

47

Edge began to shift rock fragments from off and around the carcass of the mare which was already beginning to stink with the sickly sweet stench of rotting flesh. His gear and that of Pedro were still where they had been left when the horses were unsaddled. There had been no reason to move them. One of the canteens was crushed, its contents spilled. This was the only real damage done.

The half-breed saddled Pedro's gelding and as he checked the cinch after lashing the bedroll in place, he heard Mexican voices at the other end of the cutting, beyond the debris of the rockfall.

It was safer to lead the horse by the reins along the base of the undamaged cliff face, over a strip of rock-littered trail.

"Evening, gentlemen," he said to the group of ten uniformed men who continued to sit their saddles as they gazed at the heap of rubble.

Hands moved to holsters or fisted around the frames of booted carbines. But no guns were drawn as the *Federales* watched the tall, lean man lead the horse out onto open ground.

"*Señor,*" the man with captain's insignia on his tunic said. And said in English, "You have had a narrow escape, it seems?"

"Sure did, feller."

The officer, sergeant, corporal and five enlisted men, all weary-eyed and travelstained, were surprised to see him, and suspicious of him.

"You have come far tonight?" the thinfaced captain asked as the half-breed swung up astride the unfamiliar horse.

"I've been here since evening."

"We are seeking five men. Mexicans. Bandits. They attempted to rob the bank at Fronteras six days ago. They failed, but they killed four innocent people. Have you seen five Mexicans, *señor*?"

Edge jerked a hooked thumb toward the rock pile as he rolled a cigarette between the thumb and fingers of

48

the other hand. "Pedro, Jesus, Juan, Ramon and one they called the boy."

"That is them!" the captain exclaimed, as his men expressed excited interest. "Do you mean they are underneath all that?"

"Yeah."

The captain grinned and the others matched his expression. The knowledge did not lessen their weariness, but it replaced tension with contentment.

"They deserved it," a man growled, and spat.

"The one called Ramon sure did," Edge answered. "He shot my horse."

The captain swung down to the ground. "We will camp here tonight," he told his men in their native tongue. Then, in English to Edge, "I do not disbelieve you, *señor*. But unless we dig out the bodies and take them back to the post, my commandant will not be satisfied."

"Suit yourself, feller," the half-breed answered. "I'm satisfied."

The sergeant, who was in his late fifties and showed he had stiff joints by the way he dismounted, looked hard at Edge. "I think, *señor*," he said slowly, "that all this did not happen merely by chance."

"I had more luck than I counted on," came the even-voiced reply, which drew every eye toward the only mounted man.

"*Señor?*" the captain posed.

"Like I said, one of them shot my horse. I've got a long way to ride and one of them had a horse. This one. Couldn't get restitution without killing all five of them."

"*Que* restitution?" a young *Federale* asked, speaking the syllables of the English word slowly.

"*Tapar la boca!*" the sergeant snarled. Then, in a rasping tone to Edge, "For a horse, you did all this, *señor?*"

The non-com spread his arms to encompass the massive heap of debris.

The half-breed struck a match on his boot and lit the

49

cigarette. Then showed his teeth in a cold grin as he glanced over his shoulder. "Like I say, I had a little luck, feller. But it seems that when I want something bad enough, I can move mountains."

The Battle

In the Epilogue of The Final Shot, *the last of the war flashback titles, there are a few lines which state that as a part of General Sheridan's victorious army . . . his (Captain Hedges) troop blazed the trail west along the route of the Southside Railroad—to Burkville, Farmville and then to Appomattox. Resistance was sporadic, but fierce when it occurred.' This is the story of one such encounter.*

IT was the evening of April 5 in the year 1865. The Battle of Five Forks was over and there was a strong rumor on every front that soon the war itself would be finished. But the seven men in Union cavalry uniform riding north west from Burkville, Virginia with the tracks of the Southside Railroad to their right had been soldiers for too long to set much store by rumors.

At the head of the short column was the twenty-nine-year-old Captain Josiah C. Hedges, a lean but solidly built man with jet black hair and piercing, cold blue eyes.

Immediately behind him rode Sergeant Frank Forrest and Trooper Billy Seward, respectively the eldest and youngest member of the troop.

The non-com was in his early thirties, as tall as the captain but not so broadly built. A one-time bounty hunter in the southwestern territories and Mexico, he had a mean-looking face which showed crooked and tobacco-stained teeth when he grinned or, more often, sneered.

51

Seward was just out of his teens and had a deceptively baby face. He giggled a lot, especially at other people's misfortunes, and he particularly enjoyed watching men or women die badly.

In back of these two rode Troopers John Scott and Roger Bell and at the rear were Corporal Hal Douglas and Trooper Bob Rhett. All were in their mid-twenties and with the exception of Rhett shared a similar mid-Western background with Hedges and Seward—they came from immigrant farming stock. All, too, like the youngest trooper and the captain had learned fast from the lessons of war how to kill without compunction in order to survive.

Rhett was the odd man out in the group for a number of reasons. A tall, lean, shallowly handsome man with bright eyes set in clean-cut features, he spoke with a cultured Bostonian accent and had the foppish manner of an undoubted homosexual. He was also a craven coward—the other members of the troop could never be accused of being this—who, as is so often the case with such men, became a brutal monster whenever he had a helpless victim at his mercy.

The column rode at an easy pace through the lightly falling rain, their tunics protected by regulation waterproof capes draped over their shoulders. Under the slickers they were garbed in regulation uniforms and, except for Hedges, carried army-issue Colt revolvers and knives in their belts and Spencer carbines in the boots slung from their saddles.

The captain had a Remington sixgun and a Henry repeater, a knife and a sabre. He also carried a straight razor in a pouch at the nape of his neck.

Because they had seen no action throughout this day as they scouted ahead of the Union advance on Rebels retreating from Petersburg, the troopers were smartly turned out. The horses were a little muddy from the wet ground and the men had a twelve-hour growth of stubble on their faces but, although Captain Hedges insisted on a high standard of smartness, he did not demand the impossible. And so, as he cast a backward glance over this nucleus of men whom he had commanded throughout almost the entire war, he vented a low grunt of satisfaction.

If General Robert E. Lee should appear in front of him now and offer to surrender the army of Northern Virginia, Hedges considered that he and his men were in a fit state to accept the capitulation with suitable dignity.

"Frig this stinkin' rain!" Roger Bell snarled to Scott at his side, as the troop approached an extensive stand of timber through which the railroad plunged as if into a tunnel.

Scott spat at the already-sodden ground.

"Certainly does get a man down," Rhett added. "I'm wet through."

"How do you know what gets a *man* down?" Bell countered harshly.

"Specially wet between your legs, Bob," Scott growled. "Comes from ridin' behind so many good-lookin' fellers."

"Hey, I bet he's been comin' all the lousy day!" Seward put in shrilly, giggled and drew guffaws from Bell and Scott.

"You crazy lunkheads want somebody to blow a friggin' bugle as well?" Forrest snarled and raked his small, mean eyes from Seward to the other men who had contributed to the boredom-relieving exchange.

"What's the matter, Frank?" the youngest trooper asked, petulant at the rebuke from the only man in the world he admired and respected.

"He means there could be half the Reb army in these woods, that's what!" Corporal Douglas snapped. "If we had a bugler he could sound the advance and make real sure every last one of the bastards knew we was close by."

As a vocal silence descended over the men behind him. Hedges allowed himself a brief and tight smile into the darkness of the trees ahead.

Frank Forrest had many drawbacks as a sergeant. Of most concern throughout the war had been the constant danger that he might choose to kill his commanding officer instead of the enemy he was sworn to fight. And for most of the time it was clearly apparent that it had been a mistake to promote Douglas to possibly the worst corporal in the entire Union army. But when the situation called for it, Forrest was able to call upon his innate qualities of leadership and, taking his cue from the sergeant, Douglas was able to exert authority over the men.

Now the troopers, lulled into a false sense of security by a day without danger, were abruptly tense and watchful, ignoring the discomforts of the weather and their weariness. Too keyed up, maybe.

"Please, sirs, will you help my ma?"

Before the plea was half-completed, every man had reined his gelding to a halt and fisted a hand around the frame of a booted rifle. By the time it was completed, Rhett, Douglas and Seward had slid the weapons out, cocked and leveled them. At a target who stepped out from the pitch darkness of the dripping trees to stand between the faintly gleaming rails of the railroad track. It was a boy of about twelve, tall and emaciated, his skinny frame clad in a white shirt and dark pants. He was hatless and shoeless, a Negro, the water-sheened blackness of his face emphasizing the stark whiteness of his eyes and teeth displayed in terror as the three rifle muzzles swung toward him.

"Don't kill me, sirs!" he begged, pushing both arms out in front of him, palms tilted upwards and fingers splayed. "My ma's in real bad trouble."

"Nigger, your troubles were almost all over," Seward rasped and slid the Spencer back in the boot.

"Tell it, boy!" Hedges instructed, retaining his grip on the booted Henry as his narrowed eyes swung in their sockets, trying to penetrate the darkness of the timber, not yet trusting the youngster's opening plea.

The boy lowered his right arm and arced his left to point northward. "The soldiers came to Peatville, sirs. This afternoon. Hundreds of them. Maybe thousands —I ain't good at stuff like that. The soldiers of the

South. They killed my pa. All the other Negroes. Except for Ma and me. Told the whites to go. That the soldiers of the North was comin'. My ma, she was shot here." He interrupted his fast-spoken words to indicate that his mother had a stomach wound. Then continued, faster than before so that he stammered with some words and ran others together. "But we hid in the cellar until they was all gone away. I stayed with my ma for a long time, 'cause I thought she was gonna die and I wouldn't want to leave her alone. But then I got to thinkin' she'd be all right. If she was helped. So I come to look for help. Stop a train, maybe. You sirs are soldiers who know about wounds, maybe?"

"Where the frig's Peatville, Captain?" Forrest asked.

Hedges, satisfied that if the young black boy was part of a Rebel trap it was not yet ready to be sprung, did not have to refer to his map to supply the answer. "Two miles north of the railroad."

"That puts it about on the line Lieutenant Henderson and his boys are scoutin', don't it?" the sergeant growled.

"Some soldiers like you already been through, sirs," the boy put in hurriedly. "I was too scared to talk to them. But when I saw you comin' . . . well, Ma needs help real bad."

He was still terrified, his big eyes shifting constantly from the grim set face of one cavalryman to the next. Always they lingered longest on the lean features of the officer.

"What's a nigra woman to us?" Rhett called from the rear of the column. "It's our job to patrol the railroad."

"But we have to rest up at the end of the day, trooper," Hedges countered. "And in weather like this, I'm not about to turn down the chance of having a roof over my head."

"Then you'll come to look at my ma?" the boy asked anxiously.

"Sure, boy."

The kid started to turn. "This way."

"Hold it." The captain swung in his saddle to look

55

along the column. "You're right, Trooper Rhett. This patrol is assigned to the railroad. You'll take the first two-hour sentry duty."

"Me, on my own, sir?"

"That's right," Hedges answered and, turning his gelding sideways-on to the boy, then extended a hand. "Here, you'll ride with me."

He was reluctant, his relief at getting what he wanted temporarily subdued. But then he approached the horse and allowed himself to be lifted and set astride the saddle in front of the man.

"You'll stay here on the fringe of the timber, trooper," Hedges instructed the nervous Rhett levelly. "If the Rebs decide to backtrack on their retreat they'll do it in force and you'll hear them way off. Should that happen, you ride back along the railroad and make the report to—"

"I think you should leave another man with me, sir," Rhett complained.

"In the woods at night, alone with you, Bob?" Seward countered with mock trepidation, injecting a tone of feminine shrillness into his voice.

"If you know where this town is, sir, why don't you leave Bob the nigger kid?" Roger Bell suggested.

"Yeah, Captain," John Scott added with a terse laugh. "Rhett ain't never really been one of us. Leave him the kid and he's sure to get black-balled."

"Shut up and move out," Hedges snapped. Then, over his shoulder to the disconsolate New Englander, "In two hours, I'll have Douglas spell you, trooper."

"Why not right now?" the corporal growled quietly as he heeled his horse in the wake of the others across the railroad tracks. "Y–E–L–L–O–W B–A–S–T–A–R–D."

Rhett scowled and Scott and Bell who were also close enough to hear Douglas laughed.

"The captain said to shut up!" Forrest snarled as he and then the others were infected by Hedges' suspicion of the thick cover which enclosed them as they entered the timber.

They rode in single file now, zigzagging among the trunks in the wake of Hedges who steered his horse in response to the monosyllable directions given by the boy sho shared his saddle. Although the spread of the trees' branches provided shelter from the fine rain, from time to time the water-filled leaves would sag and spill their contents down on the men passing beneath.

Lips often opened to form the shape of a curse, but no words were spoken. Only the boy's voice, instructing *left* or *right*, sounded against the steady thud of hooves on sodden ground and the less regular splashes of water drops on hats, capes and horseflesh.

As the timber began to thin out, there was no longer any need for the boy to give directions. For a glimmer of light in the distance acted as a beacon, shining through the darkness which a few moments later was devoid of rain.

"I didn't know if I would get back, sir," the youngster explained in the same low whisper he had used since entering the timber. "I could have found soldiers different from you. In case I was killed, I left the lamp alight in the house. Perhaps men like you would've seen it."

"You're real smart, son," Hedges answered absently as he concentrated his attention on the small town which was becoming more clearly defined with each yard they covered.

It was not much of a town. A cluster of crudely built frame shacks facing each other across the narrow width of a trail which ran from east to west along the northern fringe of the timber. About twenty in all, evenly divided between each side of the trail. Beyond the single street town of Peatville was the vast acreage of a tobacco plantation. The big house could not be seen, concealed behind a screen of timber about a mile to the north and reached by an arrow-straight drive which cut between the fields from the eastern end of town.

The light shone from the front window of a shack on the north side of the street, laying a wedge of yellow across the street and into the gap between two facing shacks. Hedges peered at the section of illuminated trail from the cover of the trees over a distance of a quarter mile as he held up a hand to halt the men behind him and reined in his own horse.

"Don't look like a fun place, Frank," Seward muttered.

"Your mouth, Billy," Forrest said evenly, and watched as Hedges lifted the skinny boy out of the saddle and lowered him gently to the ground.

"What's wrong with it?" Seward asked, puzzled.

"Nothin', when it ain't open."

"Ain't you gonna come take a look at Ma, sir?" the boy asked, abruptly as afraid as he was when he first showed himself at the railroad.

"Sure, son," Hedges told him with a brief smile of reassurance as he swung down into the long grass. "But we'll leave the horses here. Wouldn't want a Rebel patrol to see them bunched on the street. Go tell your ma help's on the way, uh?"

The young Negro nodded vigorously, his mind free of doubt as he heard the softly spoken words and saw the smile, but was unaware that the warmth shown along the mouthline did not reach up into the slitted eyes which continued to survey the town. "I'll sure do that, sir. Ma and me'll be real grateful for—"

"Go to her, boy!" Forrest growled as he dismounted and signaled the others to do likewise. Then, as the boy turned and moved out of the cover of the timber, the sergeant lowered his voice and proved once again that he had an uncanny ability to sense what Hedges was thinking. "What smells, Captain?"

The well-schooled cavalry mounts remained where they stood, reins hanging toward the ground under their necks, as the tense-faced men gathered around the officer and non-com.

"The grass, but not enough," Hedges answered. Then explained, "Rain ain't been any heavier in this area than back along the railroad."

"So what?" Seward muttered. "It rained hard enough to soak us all and them houses over there—"

58

"The street in the light, lunkhead!" Forrest cut in, voice low but harsh. "The nigger brat said hundreds or maybe thousands of men came through this crap town. Take a real heavy rain storm to wash out the sign that many would leave."

"I never trusted that little black bastard from the start," Hal Douglas rasped, and unbuttoned his holster flap.

"Leave it be!" Hedges hissed, now shifting his narrow-eyed gaze away from the single-street town toward which the boy was moving at a fast walk through the two-foot-high grass and weeds.

"Plan, Captain?" Forrest asked.

"You, Seward and Douglas come in from the east. South side of the street. I'll take Scott and Bell and advance from the west. North side if we can make it. Move."

He went to his horse, draped his cape over the saddle and slid the Henry from the boot. The others took their cue from him in more than mere physical actions. Their expressions were a match for the impressive set of his own and he knew from experience that the men's mental processes during the immediate future would follow a similar line to his own. For they were of the same killer's breed as he.

Frank Forrest had gotten a head start on all of them while killing for bounty money out west. But the captain and the troopers had proved to be adept students at the lessons of war. Adept and eager, enjoying the nervous tension of the build-up to slaughter and then relishing the fighting and the killing.

So Hedges paid scant attention to the men who trailed him along the fringe of the timber, then went down behind him and bellied in his wake out into the grass and weeds. And he spared no thoughts for Forrest, Seward and Douglas. In any other situation he would not have trusted any of them with a dud penny, let alone his life. But in such a situation as this, with a chance of a kill-or-be-killed battle in the offing, they trusted his leadership. And he therefore had faith in them as the meanest bunch of killers that ever wore Union blue.

The cover of grass and weed ran out some twenty feet behind the crudely built shacks on the southern side of the street. It had been cut down by plantation slaves so that they could use their back lots to grow vegetables. For at least one summer and winter the patches had been neglected, but wild vegetation had been re-established only in scattered clumps.

At the edge of the thick cover, the captain halted his snaking progress and Scott and Bell moved forward to flank him.

"That little nigger is sure actin' like all ain't well, sir," Scott hissed.

The closer the boy got to the single-street town, the more nervous he became. He shortened his stride and dragged his feet. Constantly clenched and unclenched his fists. And his head was never still as he switched his attention from the house with the lamp in the window to the timber behind him and back again. His mouth remained firmly closed now, but even across a distance of half the street's length, Hedges and the two troopers were able to see the whites of his eyes at each backward glance.

Then, just before he was about to go from sight between the two shacks into the gap illuminated by the lamp, he halted, turned, and raised both hands to cup them around his lower face. There was a quiver and a shrillness of terror in his voice when he shouted:

"Hey, ain't you soldiers comin'.."

"Floyd!" a woman screamed. "No!"

The young Negro's bare feet seemed rooted to the spot. But he turned from the waist to stare toward the house across the street as the lamp was suddenly doused.

"You was right, Mr. Hedges," Roger Bell rasped between teeth bared in a grin of evil anticipation.

The words were punctuated by a fusillade of gunshots accompanied by the shattering of glass. And for perhaps two seconds the night was lit by muzzle flashes like sheet lightning coming from the earth instead of the sky.

One such flash had its source at the edge of the undergrowth at the eastern end of town. The shot was fired by Forrest, or by Seward or Douglas on the order of the sergeant. For neither the trooper nor the corpoal would have had the nerve or intelligence to act without instruction.

But upwards of a dozen rifles were exploded from the other side of the street. Whether with the intention of blasting the young Negro to death or not, it was impossible to say. Whichever, it was not just a single bullet from a Union Spencer that tunneled through his scrawny body. Many more smashed through his flesh, sinews, muscles, bones and organs with enough impact to lift him off his feet and hurl him at least a yard from the spot where he had been standing, and fling him to the ground, the jolt of his landing causing the already-flowing blood to spurt from his many wounds.

He would have felt nothing after the touch of the first lethal bullet. Certainly he had no time to scream before he died.

Hedges, Scott and Bell did not waste precious time in watching yet another fellow human being die. For even before the boy, now a corpse, started to collapse, the captain was up and running and the two troopers were hard on his heels. All of them moved in a half-crouch, rifles held two-handed with the hammers cocked, eyes fixed upon the initial objective of the last house on the south side of the street's western end.

The trio took advantage of the covering fire provided by the three Union cavalrymen at the eastern end of town. Forrest, Seward and Douglas were all blasting shots along the street now, responding to the fusillade aimed at them from the men in the house which had once had a lamp in the window, these men now aware that their plan had gone wrong. Their enemies were no longer in the trees where the boy's shouted words had seemed to pinpoint them.

A glance to the right just before he achieved the

61

cover of the frame house showed Hedges that Forrest, Seward and Douglas were also making fast time across a back lot, firing wildly on the run. Because of the angle and the intervening buildings, the three Union troopers were in little danger of being hit, and for the same reasons had scant chance of their own bullets finding the house where the abortive trap had been laid.

But the exchange of fire was not futile. It drew the attention of the men in the house to just one end of the street. So that while these men continued to blast at attackers they could hear but not see, the other three blue-uniformed figures were able to race across the street and reach cover on the north side, rifles cold and unfired in their sweat-sticky hands.

One of the Union men saw the captain and two troopers cross the street. Hedges knew this the moment he, Scott and Bell lunged into fesh cover and the rifle fire faltered and was stilled. For he knew the way the mind of Frank Forrest worked.

The viciously tough non-com had used his initiative to good account. He had been prepared to accept responsibility for the death of the helpless Negro boy in order to create a diversion so that Hedges and the two troopers with him could reach their position unseen by the enemy.

Now it was the officer's turn to make a positive move as effective or more so than the opening attack on the men in the house. The trust the men had in Hedges was only good for as long as he proved himself a superior leader to Forrest. The moment he slipped in their estimation—and there had been a number of occasions during the war when he had come close to this—they would transfer their allegiance from the captain to the sergeant, who would have no hesitation in accepting it. For Frank Forrest hated taking orders and never had done so from any man before Hedges whom he made the exception because of a grudging respect for the captain—grudging to the extent that he never lost an opportunity to test the man, eager to see him fail. Keenly anticipating the excuse this would give him to establish his supremacy the best way there was—to his mind. By killing Captain Josiah C. Hedges.

John Scott and Roger Bell were as aware as Hedges himself that this was the latest of many tests Forrest had set. It showed on their darkly bristled faces as they looked expectantly at the captain in the total silence which followed the ending of gunfire. He did not have to search more deeply into their expressions to know they were hopeful he would fail. For, like Seward and Douglas, Rhett and Forrest, they shared the common soldier's dislike of officers. It was nothing personal. They all simply hated the authority which came with officers' braid.

"Around the rear," Hedges rasped, and stayed flat to the wall as he turned the angle of the side and back walls of the shack.

The troopers followed him, setting down their booted feet as if walking on thin ice. With no covering fire from the far end of the street, all three knew that the enemy were doubtless peering toward other areas of Peatville now, suspecting that the burst of frenetic shooting had been a diversionary tactic. But no shots exploded from the house four away from that which the trio of Union troopers were using as cover.

The buildings on the north side of the street had back lots as neglected as those opposite. But instead of a mixture of long grass and weeds behind, there was the vast expanse of fields covered with a crop of tobacco. A slight breeze rippled the fields in some areas, under a sky that was lightening as the rain clouds thinned.

"Why they all holed up in just the one place, sir?" Scott asked in a rasping whisper as Hedges led the two men to the rear of the second house along the street.

Hedges turned, tapped Scott on the shoulder and then jerked a thumb into the air. "Up on the roof and wait until the crap starts to fly, trooper," he murmured.

"Smells like it already has," Bell growled, returning his attention to Hedges after giving the scowling Scott a boost up onto the rear of the shack's low-pitched roof.

The familiar sickly-sweet smell of decomposing flesh

was not strong, but it was unmistakable to the nostrils of such men as these. It seemed to permeate the entire single-street town, just discernible along with the fresher, much pleasanter scents of wet earth and grass, timber and growing tobacco.

"Sir," Bell called softly as they reached the next shack along the street and he was given the signal to climb onto the roof.

"Yeah, trooper?" Hedges rested his rifle and cupped both hands so that Bell could place a foot in them and be raised aloft.

Bell waited until he was crouched on the roof. "You didn't answer John's question."

"That's because I don't know the answer," the captain growled, retrieved the Henry repeater and took one more look across the back lots of the shacks before he moved along the side of the one on which Bell was positioned.

All the crude dwellings of the plantation slaves were identical, with a door and two windows at the front and a door and one window at the rear. So, if the men who lured the Union patrol to Peatville feared there was a move to surround them, they should have at least tried to sneak some of their number out of the back door.

Then again, Hedges pondered with a narrowing of his eyes and a tightening of his mouthline, they should never have concentrated all their firepower in a single building in the first place.

Maybe they hadn't.

Ever since he, Scott and Bell had crossed the street without drawing fire, he had been conscious of the possibility that he and his men were advancing into a well-laid trap that took account of the very moves they were making.

The two troopers on the roofs were aware of this, too. Which was why their keen readiness to begin the killing had been blunted, by fear of the unknown.

The tall, lean Union cavalry captain crossed the gap to the shack next to the one where he knew some of the enemy were located. And, his back pressed to the rough timber, he took short side-steps along the front of it.

He knew that his own men could see him. Scott and Bell on the roofs on this side of the street. Forrest, Seward and Douglas inside or concealed by the walls of shacks across the street.

But what of the enemy?

As a fusillade of rifle shots exploded, Josiah C. Hedges felt his lips curl back to show his teeth in an expression that was a mixture of relief, triumph and self-anger.

Every shot cracked out from the shattered windows of the single shack, every bullet aimed across the street toward the area where the riflemen had known their enemy to be.

"Come on, you Yankee bastards!"

"Yeah, you all come and get us!"

"Die, blue-bellies!"

"You ain't gonna win this stinkin' war!"

After the initial volley of shots which ripped the silence to shreds, the men in the shack began to yell the taunts. Hatred gave their voices a harsh shrillness which served to make every word sound distinctly despite the constant barrage of gunfire.

Hedges, the sweat of tension drying cold on his flesh, continued to side-step across the front of the shack. Then turned and took three long strides to cross the open area and reach the corner of the building in which the enemy were gathered. This as the rifle fire ceased to be concentrated on one area, the barrels raking to left and right so that the entire south side of the street was sprayed with bullets.

The captain's expression was now of evil pleasure. He had run a high risk and whatever the outcome of this battle of Peatville, he could claim victory in the latest of another kind of battle. Against the men he commanded and against himself.

"Let's go get 'em, boys!"

"Kill the sonsofbitches!"

"Show 'em the south ain't done yet!"

The door of the shack was wrenched open. And gray uniformed figures plunged out into the night, exploding rifle shots on the run and covered by a constant barrage of fire from the glassless windows to either side of the doorway.

Hedges' Henry was leveled from the hip and he squeezed the trigger and saw a Rebel soldier tumble as he pumped the action to jack another shell into the breach.

Another Rebel staggered and pitched forward as Scott and Bell sent bullets angling down from the rooftops.

Both men hit the ground with bloodstains blossoming across the backs of their uniform tunics.

This left four still on their feet. On the run, but with less wild fervor than before, glancing over their shoulders in shock at the realization that two of their number had been backshot.

"Shit, we been tricked!"

"Damn 'em to hell!"

Hedges heard these taut-voiced comments during a brief lull in the covering fire as the men in the shack adjusted to the new situation.

Then three shots cracked out from the south side of the street, accompanied by the shattering of broken glass.

"The friggin' south's goin' friggin' west!" Billy Seward yelled in high glee as two more Rebels fell, rolled and became still on the street.

As the two survivors swerved to angle across the street in different directions, the Rebels in the shack intensified their covering fire. They sent a hail of bullets toward the windows which had been shattered by Forrest, Seward and Douglas.

Just as he had happened a few moments ago, Scott and Bell elected to aim at the same target, the nearest one. And a fifth Rebel died from two bullets tunneling into his back.

The remaining running man got off another shot and took two more strides. Then something came spinning out of the window of the shack where Frank Forrest was positioned. And the running man came to a halt, flung away his rifle, looked down at the knife buried in his belly and wrapped both hands around the hilt.

He tugged at the knife and screamed.

"Aw, quit bellyachin', Reb!" Forrest yelled, and triggered a revolver shot out through the window.

It was a heart shot that killed the man on his splayed feet and sent him into a backward fall.

Hedges heard the shots and the screams and the shouts but he did not see who or what caused them. For after making the one kill he whirled and ran along the side and around to the rear of the Rebel-held shack.

He had been seen to be taking a high risk and that was important in terms of his personal battle. For until then, Frank Forrest had been winning all the way down the line. At the outset, back at the point where the railroad entered the timber, it had been obvious there was a chance the Negro boy was part of a Rebel trap. And had the former bounty hunter been in command, the youth of Floyd would not have given the boy the benefit of the doubt. His interrogation would not have been gentle.

Forrest had not commented on Hedges' handling of the situation and from that moment the test was in progress. The captain had for a time been in grave danger of failing, after the sergeant started the shooting and revealed to the men that he had no compunction about killing young Floyd. The men were keyed up then, eager to do some killing of their own and looked to Hedges for the opening.

But the situation called for patience. A waiting game to play on the nerves of the Rebels until human nature forced them to reveal their strength and positions. But the men under the captain's tenuous command were ill-suited for such a tactic. They had smelled blood and were hungry to spill more.

This was why he had set himself up as a sweating target, against his better judgment but conscious of the

67

personal conflict that was as dangerous as the impending fight with the Rebels.

And fortune smiled on him.

Thus had he felt relief that the enemy were concentrated in one building and that their nerve had broken after such a short time, triumph at having topped Frank Forrest's play, and self-anger that he felt it necessary to compete with his own men as well as the Rebels. But at least self-anger was better than self-pity.

Now, as he gestured for Scott and Bell to join him, and moved along the rear of the house before the two troopers had started to leap down from the roofs, the grin of pleasure was firmly fixed to his lean, dark-skinned features. For he was as one with his men now. All side issues were dispensed with and he could indulge his own taste for slaughter.

He killed for the second time this day as he turned in front of the rear door of the shack and saw it flung open even as he drew back a leg to kick at it.

"Sonofa—" the man on the threshold started, but had the curse curtailed by a bullet driving into his throat and bursting clear at the nape of his neck.

Cries of alarm were amplified by the confines of the one-room shack. The vocal sounds replacing the cracks of rifle shots as men at the front doorway and flanking windows whirled.

Hedges received a fleeting image of at least six men in the process of whirling around. He shot one as he pitched forward, jacked a fresh shell into the breech as he went down and fired again as he hit the ground. Then he powered into a roll to the side, out from under a volley of shots that dug divots of earth along the stretch of earth he had been sprawled on.

"Crazy bastard!"

Hedges recognized the voice of Bell, saw the man skid to a halt, fire into the shack and then leap over him. Then Scott rushed around behind where the captain got onto all fours and blasted a shot into the window.

68

"Enough, frig it, enough!" a man shrieked above the cries and groans of the wounded.

"Takes two to make a truce!" Scott snarled, drew his revolver and started to fan the hammer, standing at the shattered window and raking the Colt to left and right.

"And there's two here ain't makin' one, Rebs!" Bell augmented, and moved onto the threshold.

He drew his revolver, as well, but was more deliberate in the way he cocked the hammer and squeezed the trigger, picking out his targets by the sounds of their pain in the dark interior of the shack.

The final shot cracked as Hedges got to his feet, flared nostrils stinging with the acrid taint of exploded powder which now masked the stench of old death and the scents of wet country. There had been time to order a ceasefire before the two Colts rattled empty, but no part of his mind had demanded he give it. Helpless as the trapped and wounded Rebels were, Floyd had been worse off.

"Hey, Frank, Billy, Hal!" Scott yelled. "You can come outta your hidey-holes now!"

"Watch your mouth, trooper!" Forrest snarled.

"The captain okay, John?" Billy Seward called with no hint of concern in his voice.

"You men check the rest of the buildings in town!" Hedges ordered as he brushed by Bell to cross the threshold of the shack.

"Sounds like his old uppity self, Billy," Douglas growled in a stage whisper he knew would carry across the street.

"Do like the man tells you!" Forrest snapped and thus acknowledged that the regulation chain of command was still established.

"Bell, you check some of the shacks," Hedges instructed. "Scott, go bring the horses out of the timber."

There were no complaints with the assignments, for familiarity had bred contempt in the matter of looking at bullet shattered corpses.

There were eight of them sprawled in the shack: one by the front door; two under each of the flanking win-

69

dows; and three piled up in a heap at the center of the floor.

Hedges saw them in the flaring light of a match he struck on the stock of the Henry and held aloft. Then, as Forrest entered through the front door, wiping the blood of a dead man from the blade of his reclaimed knife on a pants leg, both men reacted to a low moan.

Forrest crouched and drew back the knife, ready to throw it. While Hedges turned from the waist and swung the cocked rifle one-handed.

"If that's the kid's ma, he told some of the truth, Captain," the sergeant rasped.

The black woman was sprawled on her back at the foot of the shack's rear wall. Her wrists were tied together and a length of rope was taut between the bindings and a nail hammered into the front of a big grandfather clock a foot away from and a foot above her head. Other nails had been driven into the floor and bent over at each side of her ankles, forcing her to remain supine and to keep her legs splayed.

She was naked. About forty years old, her face too gaunt to be pretty and her body as scrawny as that of Floyd.

"Sure is in trouble," Forrest added as the match went out.

Hedges did not light another one. There was nothing else to see besides the woman who had been physically damaged only by countless assaults on her defenseless body, the sprawling corpses of the Rebel soldiers and the spartan furnishings of the shack—a table and four chairs made of unfinished timber, a pot-bellied stove, three mattresses and the out-of-place grandfather clock.

"My son, he is dead," the woman said, her tone injecting just the hint of a hopeful query as Hedges dropped to his haunches beside her.

"Yes, ma'am," the captain answered.

"Just some dead niggers in a few of the hovels, Frank," Billy Seward reported as he reached the threshold of the shack.

"They made him do it," the woman said.

70

"We got us a live one?" Seward asked.

"Shut up," Forrest rasped.

"Captain!" Hal Douglas yelled from the eastern end of the street.

"Go see what he wants, Sergeant."

"You are Mr. Lincoln's men?" the woman asked. "Like the others."

"Which others, ma'am?"

"Hey, you want some light on the subject, sir?" Seward asked.

"Maybe get some if you button your lip, trooper," Hedges answered in a tone of menace.

Seward spat noisily before he swung away from the doorway.

"They came at noon, the soldiers in gray. Sent the master and his people away from the big house. Said the soldiers of Mr. Lincoln were comin'. Floyd and me, we hide. Watch as they kill all us black people. My man, too. Then we are found. They use me while Floyd is watchin'. Then warned by guard soldiers of Mr. Lincoln come. Hide bodies of our people and say they will fight to death. But none die. Kill all but one of soldiers of Mr. Lincoln. He tells them more of his kind are comin'. He has to tell them this. If he does not, they say they will kill Floyd and make him eat the warm flesh of my son."

Footfalls and horses' hooves sounded out on the street.

"Captain, we found—" Forrest started.

"Henderson and his patrol," Hedges finished.

"She's talkin', uh?"

"Keeps her from thinking, feller."

"They kill him after he tells this," the woman went on in the same dull monotone as before. "Then make Floyd go to fetch you here. Say that if he does not do this, he will have to eat my flesh and drink my blood. All this I tell is the truth. Is there more that you want to know?"

Hedges came slowly upright. "No, ma'am," he answered.

71

"You gonna fill us in, Captain?" Forrest asked.

"They were a remnant of Lee's army who decided to make a stand is all," Hedges answered. "Lieutenant Henderson walked into their trap. We didn't." He turned and headed for the door. "Set the woman free."

"No!" she cried, and there was emotion in her voice for the first time since she yelled across the street into the night. Then it was gone again. "My men died here. My son. And all our people. I want my defiled body to die here, too. Please."

Captain Hedges had an impulse to try to talk the woman out of her misery. But from the doorway, breathing night air that now smelled only of old and new death, he abruptly felt too weary to nurture the spark of compassion into full life.

He raked his slitted eyes around the faces of the killers in uniform arced in front of the shack. Then, "Guess there's no problem in getting a volunteer. Make it quick for her."

Seward stepped forward, drawing his Colt.

"Nah, don't waste lead," Forrest growled and went into the shack behind the youngest trooper.

As Scott, Bell and Douglas crowded onto the threshold, Hedges swung up astride his gelding and booted the Henry rifle.

The woman had time to scream. Then there was a heavy thud, a tinkle of breaking glass, a splintering of wood and a clash of displaced metal.

The three men in the doorway moved away and Forrest and Seward emerged from the shack, looking satisfied and brushing dust from their hands.

"Mission accomplished, Captain," the sergeant reported. "Pushed that friggin' heavy clock on her."

"Yeah, I heard," Hedges answered as he dug the makings from a pocket of his tunic and began to roll a cigarette. "Guess for the kind of hurt she had, time really was a great healer."

Chapter Three

WHEN Edge woke at sun up the day after his run-in with the Mexican bandits it was the same as almost every other time since the opening weeks of the War Between the States. The few exceptions were when he had bedded down sick or with too much rye whiskey under his belt.

So when he snapped open his eyes and looked up into the no-longer pitch-blackness of the underside of his hat, he knew instantly where he was and had total recall of how he got there. Thus, as he folded up into a sitting posture and tipped the Stetson onto the top of his head, turning first one way and then the other to rake his hooded eyes over his surroundings, he was not a man trying to establish bearings. Instead, he was checking to see that he had come awake naturally and that his mind was not triggered to awareness by its highly developed sixth sense for menace.

But the brush-covered hillside on which he had made camp was silent and still in the post-dawn warmth and light of the rising sun. Except for small sounds and weary movements made by the scrawny gelding foraging on a tether twenty feet or so higher up the incline.

Above where the horse stood, the rise reached to a rocky ridge which was starkly outlined against the solid blueness of the northern sky. A mile to the west and half that distance in the east, the ridge made almost right-angle turns to run southwards down the slope. The outlaw trail from Paraiso emerged from behind the rocky arm in the east and was visible for several miles on the desert-like terrain which spread southwards toward a line of craggy rises and steep-sided mesas.

This meant the half-breed had needed to doubleback some in order to bed down on the slope. But there was time enough to take such precautions and even though the night had past peacefully, the man did not consider the spare time had been used wastefully.

While he lit a small fire, boiled water for coffee and cooked a breakfast of salt pork and beans, he continued to make use of his carefully chosen vantage point to keep watch over his surroundings. Just once, a memory of the long-ago war flitted through his mind. Sparked by the appearance of the *Federale* patrol, the column of men riding into view from behind the ridge in the southeast.

The captain at the head of the column saw the smoke of Edge's fire, swung in his saddle and raised fieldglasses to his eyes. The half-breed, a cup of coffee to his lips, lifted a hand and touched the brim of his hat with a forefinger. The captain lowered the binoculars and responded to the greeting with a weary wave of his arm, then, like his men, lost the scant interest in Edge which all had shown for a short time. Weary from the night-time chore of shifting rocks to recover the bodies of the crushed bandits, the column moved out across the desert. Most of the men rode with a blanket-wrapped corpse lashed to their bedrolls.

Edge drank another cup of coffee and smoked a cigarette, giving the patrol time to ride more than a mile out into open country, under a rising sun that beat down with a harsher light and a more fierce heat by the moment. Then, after he had broken camp, saddled and mounted the gelding, the *Federales* had gone from sight, lost behind a veil of their own dust and a shimmering heat haze.

Back on the trail himself, riding slowly over the sign left by the *Federales*, Edge again thought briefly of the war. He touched the shirt pocket in which the letter rested. The letter that referred to an incident in the past which had made it difficult for him to get to sleep last

night while his subconscious tried to force him to remember and relive in vivid detail the pain and anger
and anguish of that blackest of times. Until a random
thought of the *Federale* captain and his men success-
fully concluding a patrol had triggered an easier-to-
sleep-with memory of other soldiers in different uniforms in another country achieving what they set out to
do. One soldier in particular.

A little before midday the half-breed reached a fork
in the trail, in front of a low but expansive wedge-
shaped mesa with a trickling spring four feet above the
base of its point. The sign showed that the *Federales*
had halted here to water their horses before moving off
again along the south-west spur.

Edge dismounted, half-filled his hat from the spring,
allowed the gelding to drink and then repeated the
process. He drank himself, topped up his canteen with
the warm but reasonably sweet water and then tipped
half a hatful over his head, relishing the feel of the run-
nels coming out of his hair and coursing down his
darkly bristled face.

There was not much shade from the thirty-feet-high
northwest face of the mesa, but the presence of running
water made it a good enough place to rest up for a
while after the long morning's ride in the sun. So he
uncinched the saddle, placed it at the base of the mesa
and lowered himself gratefully onto it, resting his back
against the rough rock. The dispirited horse stood in the
patch of shade into which he had been led, statuelike
except for the slow rise and fall of the belly as he
breathed. He did not even lift his head and prick his
ears when, against the sound of trickling water, the clop
of slow-moving hooves could be heard.

Two or maybe three shod horses were being ridden
toward the point of the mesa up the trail spur from the
south east no more than fifteen minutes after the half-
breed had lowered himself onto the saddle.

Now, a freshly lit cigarette hanging from the side of
his mouth, he rose to his feet and slid the Winchester
from its boot. He canted the rifle to his left shoulder as

he stepped around the angle of rock, halted beside the patch of shingle through which the spring water soaked away.

"Hey, Jack, there's a guy up ahead!"

The woman's voice was shrill with fear, her words clearly heard in the Sierra Madre stillness even though she and the two men riding either side of her were more than four hundred yards away.

"So what, Flo?" the man to her left countered. "Ain't nothin' to get excited about."

"The hell you say, Clyde!" Jack snarled. "You friggin' gotta know anythin' with balls between its legs gets my wife excited!"

"Up yours, husband dear!" the woman retorted.

Jack wrenched on the reins to steer his horse close to that of his wife, then swung his right hand up and to the side. As the back of his hand crashed into the underside of the woman's jaw, Clyde streaked his right hand from the saddle horn to fist it around the butt of a holstered revolver.

Flo gasped in pain and had to grasp her saddle horn to keep from being knocked backwards off her horse.

Jack leaned forward to look across the front of his wife at Clyde and rasped, "You figure it's time to make that try, old buddy?"

There had been no faltering in the progress of the three riders since the woman had spotted Edge and spoken the words which led to the blow and a threat of greater violence.

"You didn't oughta beat up on Flo like you do, Jack," Clyde complained sourly, and returned his hand to the saddle horn. "It's like you never stop insultin' her and beatin' up on her."

Jack shared a sneering stare between the man and the woman, and growled, "She's mine to do what I like with, ain't she?" and then turned his attention toward Edge. "Mornin' mister," he called. "Water still comin' outta Flecha Mesa?"

They were close enough now to see the slight nod with which the half-breed responded. Close enough for

76

Edge to see that Jack was the oldest of the trio. Pushing fifty, he was no taller than five-and-a-half feet but the flesh was packed solidly on his frame. Likewise, his round face, which at first glance seemed fat, was in fact firmly constructed, covered by leathery skin deeply inscribed with lines which all had a downward curve. He had iron-gray hair in his long sideburns and a neatly trimmed moustache. But his bristles were black.

Clyde was ten years younger, a lean six-foot tall with a long and almost gaunt face. His bristles and sideburns were red.

Both men were dressed in black Stetsons, kerchiefs, shirts, pants and spurred riding boots. Both were armed with Frontier Colts and Winchester rifles. Both astride strong-looking black stallions, sitting Western-style saddles hung with all the accoutrements necessary for a long ride over rugged country. And both, as they reined their horses to a halt ten feet from where Edge stood, looked at the half-breed with dark eyes as lacking in warmth as those of the man on the ground.

"Been a real lifesaver for a lot of men, this water," Jack said as he swung down from his saddle. "Cash is the name. Jack Cash. This here's Clyde Bodelle. Lady's my wife. Florence is her name."

"Edge," the half-breed supplied as he stepped to the side so that Cash had a clear passage to where the water came out of the rock face.

As Cash came by him, Edge smelled the sweat and dirt of his body, and the whiskey on his breath.

"You threw a real scare into me, Mr. Edge," the woman admitted as she dismounted. "Steppin' around the corner like that, that rifle held the way it is."

She was no taller than five feet, with a full figure garbed in a tight-fitting white shirt and an ankle-length black skirt with enough flare for her to ride astride a horse without revealing more than half the length of her high-buttoned boots. There was a shallow prettiness in the composition of her features, drawn largely from the big roundness of her green eyes. But at twenty-five or so she was already tending to fat and there was a dan-

77

ger that overweight might soon destroy the tenuous grip she had on voluptuous attractiveness.

Clyde, who had made to help the woman dismount, and had held back when Jack glanced harshly at him, swung down to the ground and showed a grim smile. "A man in the Sierra Madres don't take chances with strangers, Flo. Specially not along this trail."

The younger man had had his share of the whiskey, or maybe more. Certainly he was unsteady on his feet as he moved toward the spring.

"Well, you got nothin' to fear from us, Mr. Edge," Flo Cash assured the half-breed, with a smile which showed fine, white teeth. As she patted ill-cared-for hair, too yellow to be natural.

"Quit your preenin', woman!" Her husband snapped, as he turned from drinking at the spring and caught her smiling at Edge while gently exploring the bruised area under her jaw. "All the time you gotta act like a two-dollar whore when there's a man around!"

He went to his horse, using his kerchief to wipe droplets of water off his bristles. His wife scowled at his back as Bodelle half-turned away from the spring, to stare hatefully at his partner across his cupped hands filled with water.

Cash sensed the animosity and shot a grim-eyed glance back over his shoulder. Clyde Bodelle drank the water and the woman sighed and ran the back of a hand over her sweat-tacky brow.

"Come on, hurry it up, Clyde!" she urged. "I want some, too."

Edge sucked in smoke and let it out through his nostrils as Cash began to chew on a strip of jerked beef he took from his saddle bag.

"Don't say much, do you?"

"Say one thing, feller."

"What's that?"

"You people are taking care of your own needs. Horses look like they could use some water."

Cash nodded and swallowed a wad of half-chewed beef before he added, "Man don't take him a wife just so he can get laid regular, mister. Flo takes care of the horses. Say somethin' to you?"

"Sure."

Cash's neutral expression changed into a scowl. And the easy tone he had spoken in before was suddenly gone. "Mind your own friggin' business!"

Edge simply nodded.

Bodelle vented a short laugh as he extracted an unlabelled bottle from a saddlebag. "Don't mind Jack, mister," he said. "He ain't never happy unless he's grouchy."

"Damn right!" the woman agreed, a sneer in her voice. Then said joyfully, "Gee, that feels beautiful."

Cash had swung his head around to glare at Bodelle, his mouth opening to hurl a curse at the younger man. But his wife captured his enraged attention and he froze, dark eyes fixed upon her and half-open mouth displaying a wad of partially chewed beef.

Bodelle was also transfixed for part of a second, in the act of raising the uncapped bottle to his lips, his eyes fear-filled as they stared at Cash and obviously recognized the signs that his partner was about to commit a new act of violence.

Then, as both Edge and Bodelle looked toward the cause of the third man's wrath, Cash powered away from his horse.

"Like a two-dollar friggin' whore!" he bellowed.

Flo had sat down in the shingle after drinking from the spring, and leaned her back against the rock, tilting her head so that the water ran into her yellow hair, down over her face and then fell to soak her shirt and skirt.

It was the cooling effect of the water on her head and face that triggered her joy. Her husband's rage was sparked by the way the water-soaked shirt clung to her upper body, closely contouring her full breasts and the erected nipples that crested them.

For a stretched second—as she heard Cash's shout, leaned forward to come out from under the spring water, and saw the depth of anger inscribed on the face of the man—naked terror took command over every muscle and line of her features. And for that time there was a kind of beauty visible in her pathetic helplessness.

"No!" she gasped.

As Cash's large frame concealed her from the other two men and he came to an abrupt halt, stooped and reached down with both hands to grab her.

A movement on the periphery of the half-breed's vision caused his eyes to flick along the thin lines of their sockets and he was in time to see Clyde Bodelle draw, cock and level the Colt revolver.

The woman screamed as she was jerked to her feet, her husband's double-handed grip fastened in her hair. Then his right hand released her and he pulled the arm to the side and swung it back again.

"Time, you bastard!" Bodelle snarled, and hurled the whiskey bottle to the ground.

It was bluster. He looked and sounded deeply afraid. And hesitated for a fraction of a second—a man on the point of doing something he desperately wanted to do, but concerned that this new opportunity, seeming perfect, contained a hidden danger.

Cash altered the arc of his right arm, abandoned the intended blow at his wife and went for his holstered Colt. At the same time, he pivoted on his left heel and jerked harder at Flo's hair.

Bodelle's momentary hesitation was lengthened as Cash, too well built to hide behind his wife, was abruptly partially shielded by her pain-wracked writhing form.

The bigger, older man did not waste the opportunity. The instant his gun was leveled alongside Flo's hip and aimed at Bodelle's frozen form, he squeezed the trigger.

The crack of the gunshot resounded off the face of the mesa point and faded into silence across the desert.

The woman's scream was curtailed by the sight of Clyde Bodelle falling backwards against the side of his horse, a blood-stain blossoming across the front of his shirt, left of center.

The horse snorted and side-stepped, raising a cloud

of dust from beneath his hooves. Bodelle, his death mask an expression of abject disappointment, fell into the rising dust. The impact of his corpse against the ground puffed up more motes, which drifted down again and clung to the sticky blood oozing from the bullet wound.

Flo sobbed.

Edge thumbed back the hammer of the Winchester still sloped to his left shoulder. And the small sound drew Cash's eyes to him like iron filings to a powerful magnet. The eyes were as hard and unfeeling as chips of rusty metal. The man cocked his gun and turned the woman so that she was now a shield against the half-breed.

"You figure to take a hand in this, mister?" he rasped.

"Only if you try to aim that gun at me, feller," Edge answered evenly as the taint of gunsmoke was neutralized in the hot air and just the smell of spilled whiskey from the broken bottle was left. "You do that and somebody else will die here."

Cash gave a curt nod, holstered his Colt as fast as he had drawn it, and flung his wife away from him.

She screamed at the pain as the roots of her hair took the brunt of her husband's new viciousness, howled as she staggered for several feet, struggling to remain upright, then screamed again as she sprawled into a crashing fall on her belly.

"Guess you're a whole lot smarter than that crazy Clyde Bodelle, mister," Cash said. "If any woman's worth dyin' for, she ain't the one. But if a man don't protect what's his, he ain't much of a man, wouldn't you say?"

"Say something, feller," Edge responded as Flo began to whimper and writhe on the ground, seeking to assuage her pain.

"What's that?" Suspiciously, the dark eyes fixed upon the half-breed's impassive face.

"Like to buy the dead man's horse."

Cash suddenly grinned and glanced at the stallion

which was now standing calmly beyond where the body of his former rider was crumpled. He ignored his wife who was now as silent and almost as unmoving as the dead man six feet away from where she lay.

"Ill wind, ain't it?"

"How much?"

Cash looked briefly and contemptuously at the undernourished gelding. "Guess old Clyde's mount is the only halfway decent horse around for a whole lot of miles, mister."

He was half-turned away from where his wife lay, half-turned toward Edge. Edge did not move a muscle in his face and revealed no tensing of his body as he glimpsed the woman reach out a hand toward Bodelle's discarded Colt, the hammer of which was still cocked.

"Spare me the sales talk about supply and demand, feller. How much?"

The woman had to stretch her arm to the full extent of its reach, and her fingers likewise.

"You after bounty or runnin'?"

"Neither."

She fisted a filthy hand around the butt.

"See, it's a matter of how much you can afford to pay, mister. Bounty hunter ridin' south wouldn't have much of a stake. Man on the run might be runnin' with a big roll."

"Name your price."

She lifted the gun no more than an inch above the ground and showed by the tacit plea in her eyes that she was aware Edge knew of her intention.

"Can you afford a hundred?"

"I can afford it. Ain't prepared to pay it, though."

Flo's face was tense now, sweat drops standing out from every pore as she inched her arm around. And drew a bead on the broad back of her husband.

"So no deal," Cash answered. He made to turn away from the half-breed, but was a fraction of a second too late.

The gun exploded and bucked in the fisted right hand of the woman, and sent a bullet smashing through

Cash's right hand and into his hip as he saw the aimed Colt and reached for his own revolver.

"Jesus," he rasped as the impact of the shot rocked him on his feet.

Edge took a step to the side and swung the Winchester across his chest, holding it two-handed now.

Cash made to reach across the front of himself and draw the holstered Colt left-handed. But his wife cocked Bodelle's gun and squeezed the trigger again. This bullet took Cash in the belly. The blood it erupted spread across his shirt while that from his wounded hand continued to drop to the dust.

Flo came up into a sitting position, folded her other hand around the gun butt and sent another shot across the ten feet of hot, smoke-smelling air.

Cash took another bullet in the belly, but stayed on his feet. He revealed his strength even further when he took a step toward the woman whose expression of gleeful triumph was abruptly replaced by terror.

"Help me, Edge!" she shrieked. And blasted a fourth shot at her husband.

This bullet hit higher, tearing into and through his left shoulder. It caught him in mid-stride, stopped and half-turned him. The man groaned his pain now, but changed the sound into a roar of rage as he made to advance again.

"Help me!" Flo demanded, shriller.

She screwed her eyes tight closed, cocked the hammer, squeezed the trigger, cocked and squeezed again.

The fifth shot opened up a bloody hole in his right cheek. The sixth missed him, but it was of no consequence. For like all the other bullets, the fifth one was fired on a rising trajectory; it tunneled up through his head and penetrated his brain to kill him.

For long moments after he had crashed to the ground, his widow continued to cock the hammer and squeeze the trigger of the Colt, her sobs masking the series of clicks as the firing pin hit against expended cartridges. She kept this up until Edge went to her, stooped and plucked the empty gun from her hands. Then she screamed.

"No sweat, lady," the half-breed told her. "He's dead."

She curtailed the sound of terror, opened her eyes and stared at the blood-spattered corpse of Jack Cash. At first she was incredulous. Then she grinned her triumph. Next showed a sneer to the tall, lean man towering over her.

"Thanks a whole bunch for the help," she rasped.

"Try never to get involved in family disputes," he answered, dropped the empty gun and went to take a closer look at the two stallions.

But as he examined them, and decided that the mount of Jack Cash was the best, he did not totally ignore the woman. He was aware of her as she got painfully to her feet and shared a new grin of triumph equally between the two dead men.

"Worked out like you planned or better?" he said, uncinching Cash's saddle.

She vented a short, harsh, bitter laugh. "You bet, mister. If you was a woman, would you want either of them to screw you?"

Edge took the long, dead cigarette off his lower lip and arced it to the ground. "Figure if I was a woman, I'd take more care choosing a husband, lady."

"It ain't as simple as that," she flung at him. Then moderated her tone as she watched him cross to get his own saddle, and slide the Winchester into the boot before carrying it to Cash's horse. "Where you headed, Mr. Edge?"

"Place called Mesa del Huracan."

"I know where that is. Can I come with you?"

Edge began to saddle the horse. "Trail's free to anyone who wants to ride it, lady."

"I'm free now," she said huskily, hands on her hips and body provocatively posed, following him with eager eyes as he carried his bedroll from the gelding to the stallion. Flies began to swoop toward the corpses and, high overhead, a group of buzzards started to circle.

84

"Figure they don't come any cheaper than you."

She was abruptly rigid with rage, her face suddenly dark and heavy with venomous spite. "You're as mean and evil as them two were!" she snarled with a wave of her hand to encompass the pair of bodies on which the flies were feeding. "Without an ounce of common decency in you!"

Edge sighed, nodded and swung up astride his new mount. "You and me both, I figure, lady," he muttered. "And there just ain't no peace for the wicked."

The Woman

In The Blue, The Gray and the Red *the flashback se-
quences were told how Captain Hedges and his men
were captured by the Confederates, held in Andeson-
ville Prison and began their escape bid. Chapter Eight
of that book begins: "It took Hedges six weeks to fully
recover from the effects of his initiation into Andeson-
ville . . ." What follows took place toward the end of
this period of recuperation.*

Captain Josiah C. Hedges no longer felt any pain from
the beating and the long hours of hanging by the wrists
from a framework in the center of the Andersonville
Prison stockade. This punishment, ordered by Captain
Henry Wirz, commandant of the prison, in retribution
for the Union officer's leadership of an attempted mass
escape, had been inflicted several weeks previously.
How many weeks, Hedges did not know because he had
been delirious for a great deal of the time.

Not that it mattered. Except for waking, eating and
sleeping, time was of little consequence in this hellhole
of a prison built on the edge of a Georgia swamp. He
realized this from eavesdropping on the sporadic talk
among the six men who shared the crude shebang with
him; Sergeant Frank Forrest, Corporal Hal Douglas
and Troopers Billy Seward, John Scott, Roger Bell and
Bob Rhett, a group of the meanest and most vicious
killers who had ever worn any kind of uniform in any
war anywhere.

But they did not look so tough on this morning when

Hedges came silently awake and, for the first time since he was cut down from the punishment frame, was aware of a world that existed beyond the confines of excruciating private agony.

He discovered he was lying on his back on a patch of straw against a tin wall of the shebang. The three other walls were of timber and the roof was formed of an area of canvas stretched taut across the walls. There was no door, just a hole in one of the walls through which sunlight entered, hot and bright. But not only the light of the day came in through the hole, along with the stench of swampland, human waste, bad cooking, smoke, defeat, degradation and death. These foul odors mingled with those which were generated by the seven men who shared the cramped space beneath the canvas roof.

The men seemed to have shrunk since the captain had last been aware of seeing them. Cracking his eyes against the cruel brightness of the mid-morning sun and because he did not wish the men to know he was awake and alert, he studied them for a full minute.

They had not shrunk in height, of course, but certainly they had lost a great deal of weight. None of them had ever been fat, but now leanness and strength had given way to something approaching emaciation. Their uniforms looked to be at least two sizes too big for them, the bone structures of their faces were gauntly prominent and their eyes were sunk deep in the sockets. Stubble had grown into beards and their flesh and clothing were filthy.

Each small movement they made and every brief sentence they spoke served to emphasize the low level of weakness to which incarceration and malnutrition had driven them.

And yet Hedges himself felt reasonably well. Weak, certainly, and if he elected to concentrate he could experience a dull ache in his lower belly and other areas of discomfort in muscles which had been punished by the long hours he hung on the frame. And he guessed his flesh contributed as much as anyone else's to the rancid atmosphere within the shebang. But his comparative well-being surely resulted from more than just the enforced rest . . .

"All right, Bob, go start cook' up some steaks," Forrest growled from where he lay on his back against the wall across from Hedges.

The effeminate New Englander scowled and continued to sit on his haunches beside the hole in the wall. "I wish you wouldn't make jokes about the shit grub we have to eat, Sarge," he whined.

"I wish we didn't have to give the lousy captain the best of the lousy crud we get to eat," Billy Seward rasped.

Hedges eased his eyes fully closed as Seward and Scott and Bell, leaning their backs against one of the wooden walls, shifted their hollow-eyed gazes toward where he lay.

"One more time, Billy," Forrest said as Rhett crawled wearily out through the hole. The non-com's voice was weak, but he managed to inject a familiar note of menace into his tone. "The same for all you lunkheads. Come up with an idea I think gives us half a chance to bust outta this stinkin' joint and I'll be happy to let Captain Josiah Friggin' Hedges waste away in his friggin' sleep."

"I ain't never said nothin' about—" Hal Douglas tried to interrupt.

"You ain't never said nothin' worth a friggin' damn in your whole life!" Forrest cut in on him. "Same as the rest of you guys. Hadn't been for Hedges and me lookin' out for you, not one of you would have made it through the war this far."

"Bein' dead's gotta be better than bein' here," Seward muttered.

"You really want it that way, kid, you let me know," the sergeant countered. "You lost some fat, so after I've choked you to death, we oughta be able to have us some nice lean, real steaks."

Hedges cracked open his eyes again, in time to see

Frank Forrest slide the straight razor out of the neck pouch he took from a pants pocket.

"Bob'll really go for a piece of your ass, Billy," Scott said, trying to laugh but ending up coughing.

"Choke, you bastard, choke!" Seward snarled.

As had happened several times earlier since Hedges became aware of his surroundings, the talk came to an abrupt end, the men closing their eyes, sagging their heads and slumping their shoulders, as if the mere act of uttering words sapped their already vastly depleted reserves of stamina.

Hedges closed his own eyes and expended the slight effort necessary to feign continued unconsciousness. He now knew why he did not feel so sick as the men looked and knew also that in this never-before-experienced situation, nothing had changed in his relationship with the men. They were keeping him alive because they needed him. So, for the time being, he was content. To the extent that, against the murmur of sounds which entered the shebang from the stockade beyond, he drifted involuntarily into a deep and natural sleep.

Then he came awake with a start as fingers forced his lips apart and something metallic rapped against his teeth. Instinctively he brought up his hands to defend himself and as he opened his eyes he saw only a blurred image of a man stooped over him.

"Hey, you guys, the captain's back in the land of the livin'."

Hedges recognized the voice of Forrest, then saw the haggard face of the man clearly.

"If you can call this friggin' livin'," Billy Seward growled.

The captain recalled his earlier lucid period of being awake.

"Figure you can handle it yourself," Forrest said, and thrust into Hedges' hand a tin cup. The lip on one side had been hammered out of shape to form a spout.

"What is it?" His own voice sounded reedy to him.

"Somethin' that passes for food in this shithole of a prison camp," John Scott supplied as Forrest crawled to the other side of the shebang and picked up a tin plate and joined the others in eating solid food. There were no irons, so they ate with their fingers.

Hedges rose onto one elbow and sipped at the liquid contents of the mug. It was a thick soup with a distinctive and not entirely unpleasant flavor.

"Better than we got, sir," Bob Rhett amplified without enthusiasm. "We have what the rebs give us. Always arrange something special for you."

"I'm honored," Hedges said wryly, never expecting to be asked how he felt, so not concerned by the embittered tones and soured expressions which greeted his return from prolonged unconsciousness.

"You're right not to grovel your thanks, Mr. Hedges," Forrest muttered. "You know what happened, where you are?"

The captain nodded.

"You've had it easy. Sleepin' all the time. Figure when you find out how bad it is in this lousy pigpen, you'll want out. And if anyone can get out, you can."

"Takin' us with you, of course," Hal Douglas put in.

"You bet," Roger Bell added.

The sunlight shafting through the hole in the wall was abruptly interrupted. All the men looked toward the shebang entrance, but only Hedges expressed interest after a man rasped:

"In you go."

There was a small cry, then a flurry of movement. A stooped figure staggered into the crude shack, forced by a shove from behind, and collapsed to the dirt floor with a groan that encompassed both pain and despair.

"Olsen says thanks for the loan, Mr. Forrest," the man outside called. "He can maybe use the goods again after they been patched up some."

The men laughed and moved away, so that the sunlight poured into the shebang again. Hedges could see clearly the hapless individual who had been tossed across the threshold was a figure clad only in a stinking blanket, this held in place by lengths of rope around the waist and under the armpits. The feet and lower legs and the back of the head were left uncovered, enough to cause Hedges to do a double-take.

"Yeah, you can believe what you see, Captain," Forrest confirmed. "It's female."

Like the others, the sergeant continued to chew without enjoyment on the unappetizing food totally ignoring the woman sprawled on her face in front of them.

"She ain't much," Roger Bell said, "but you oughta be real grateful to her."

"Been your meal ticket, sir," Scott added.

The woman shifted her head, turning it to the side so that Hedges was able to see her face as it emerged from among the strands of matted, long red hair. It was the face of a woman in her late twenties fixed with an expression which told silently of unspeakable suffering. A face with a broad forehead, high cheekbones and blunted jaw, with coal black eyes set deep in hollow sockets, a finely shaped nose and a thin-lipped mouth. The eyes had been cried dry of tears, the mouth was slack and gave a glimpse of discolored teeth and the dirt-ingrained skin was marked with the scars and contusions of old and more recent beatings.

The dark eyes gazed without blinking at the bearded face of the captain and he guessed the woman was trying to transmit an emotion to him but had been drained of the ability to feel anything except abject hopelessness.

"I believe what I see, Sergeant," Hedges said. "You going to tell me what I can't see?"

Forrest thrust a final piece of food into his mouth and chewed on it, grimaced as it went down his throat.

"Rebs tossed her in here two nights after the lights went out for you," he replied around his thumb which probed for a shred of something lodged in his teeth. "Said she was a Union spy and they figured passin' her around the prisoners would make her suffer more than just stringin' her up."

Hedges shifted his slitted eyes briefly to the death-like face of the punished woman but she expressed no response to Forrest's dull-voiced explanation.

"Looks like they were right."

Forrest freed the discomforting piece of food and spat it out. "Guess even the Rebs have to be right sometimes."

"Sure picked the right bunch to give her to."

"You oughta hear Frank out before you climb on your high horse, Mr. Hedges," John Scott growled.

"Yes, sir," Bob Rhett added. "If we didn't make use of the woman the way we did, you'd probably be long dead by now."

Hedges raked his eyes over the face of each of the men and then settled his gaze on the countenance of the sergeant. The grin he saw there revealed that Frank Forrest had won another play against him. He pursed his lips, lowered the back of his head to the straw and looked up at the canvas ceiling.

"You traded her body for my food, uh?"

"Yeah," Seward said, and giggled. "Guess you can say that, in a manner of speakin', you been eatin' pussy."

Nobody laughed.

"There's a man in this pigpen named Olsen," Forrest explained. "A fat slob of a prisoner who lives higher off the hog than the friggin' Rebs guardin' us. For a price, he can get anyone most anythin'. Decent food, liquor, materials to keep the rain outta the shebangs, patent medicines . . . most anythin', 'ceptin' for a woman. We got the woman, so we traded."

"After we sampled the goods ourselves, naturally," Roger Bell put in.

"Not countin' Bob, course," Scott added.

"Captain knows naturally ain't the way Bob does it," Bell came back, and brought smiles to their faces and a snort and a scowl from the effeminate New Englander.

"She was in better shape then," Forrest said with a note of remembered lust in his voice, then glanced down at the wasted, gaunt-faced woman and grimaced at her present condition.

"If you like a woman with beestings for tits and ribs that stick into your belly," Hal Douglas rasped.

Without shifting his narrow-eyed gaze from the overhead canvas, Hedges said, "Guess it won't help how you feel, ma'am, but I'm obliged to you."

"She feels fine, sir," Scott said with a leer and a flexing of his fingers. "If you ain't so friggin' particular as Hal."

"Obliged to the Walters dame, but not to us, uh?" Seward snarled.

"We already covered that, Billy," Forrest snapped. "Captain knows as well as we do we didn't nurse him back to health outta the goodness of our friggin' hearts. Wasn't on account of we love him that we went without tobacco and whiskey and meat and regular pussy ourselves just so he could—"

"You . . . " the woman started, and her voice caused Forrest to curtail his embittered words. She tried again as all attention was shifted to her. "You are the first man in this terrible place . . . to offer me a kind word, sir. It is not . . . not much, but anything is . . . something."

Her voice sounded pained and husky, as if her throat was as devoid of saliva as her eyes were of tears.

"It talked," Seward said, surprised.

"That unusual?" Hedges asked.

"She did a lot of beggin' and pleadin' when the Rebs first tossed her in here," Forrest replied. "Not much to say for herself after she started screwin' around. Prayed some for a while each time the Rebs brought her back."

"Brought her back?" Hedges asked.

Forrest recognized there was more than mere idle curiosity behind the question and he was abruptly more interested himself in the exchange.

"Yeah. Somethin' Olsen fixed up for. Every couple of days the Rebs come and get her and take her into one of the forts that guard this stinkin' prison. Give her a bath and wash her hair and that kinda stuff. They'll be by for her some time this afternoon, I guess."

"Woman that does what she has to, she gets pretty

dirtied up, you know what I mean, sir," Roger Bell augmented. "Can't change what she is, but she smells a little sweeter when she comes back in. And the sweeter she smells, the better deals Olsen can make with her."

"She sure don't smell sweet as her name now, do you, Rose?" Scott growled, pushing forward a booted foot to nudge one of her filthy ankles.

"Why can't you leave her be?" Bob Rhett snarled. "Now that she's served her purpose."

Since she had spoken to Hedges, Rose Walters had reverted to her attitude of unmoving silence, seemingly detached from her squalid surroundings—withdrawn into an imaginary world probably more nightmarish than the real one. Her leg moved like dead flesh in response to Scott's touch and she appeared not to hear the words spoken about her.

"Don't tell me what to do, you swish bastard!" Scott countered.

"Shut up, you lunkheads!" Forrest rasped, still intrigued by Hedges' thoughtful silence, but showed a cynical grin to the men who turned resentful eyes toward him, and moderated his tone. "Captain's awake, but only just. Reckon he'll need some peace and quiet for his ideas to start comin' like they always used to."

"How much peace and quiet, Frank?" Seward asked. "And for how long? I've had this shit place, up to here."

The other Union prisoners remained silent, but their tacit eagerness to get free of Andersonville was more vocal than that of the youngest trooper as they directed their hollow-eyed gazes toward Hedges.

"Maybe you'd like to take a stroll around outside to see what this place is like, sir," Rhett suggested at length.

"I've already seen, trooper," Hedges answered, and continued to look up at the canvas after a surreptitious glance at Rose Walters, who had suddenly revealed a flicker of interest in the world beyond her personal suffering.

For a few moments, Hedges did ponder on what lay

immediately outside the confines of the reeking she-bang. During this time three gray-uniformed guards approached the shack and two of them aimed rifles through the entrance while the third dragged the woman out.

The prison, as he recalled from when he and a train-load of other captured Union soldiers were brought in, sprawled close to the small village of Anderson with its South Western Railroad depot. It was sited on a swamp, encircled by a fifteen-foot-high fence of pine logs. There were four forts built outside the fence. In-side, a short distance from the foot of each fence was a length of twine, known as the deadline because any prisoner who stepped over it was assumed to be escap-ing and was shot down. The prisoners lived—or died—in tents, holes in the ground and shebangs of all kinds of contruction. From the north and only gate in the fence ran a pathway known as Main Street, with spurs going off at intervals. A stream, inappropriately called the Sweetwater River, trickled this way and that across the fenced enclosure.

"Well, Captain?" Bell asked eagerly after the woman had been hauled out of the shack. "What do you think? Any ideas?"

"Why did they give her to us?" Hedges asked, tested his ability to get up into a sitting posture and found he could make it.

"What?" Douglas asked.

"This feller Olsen is supposed to have all the pull. So why did the Rebs give Rose Walters to us?"

They all looked at Forrest, who allowed a grin to spread across his face, so that the gaunt, bearded fea-tures of the former bounty hunter seemed to glow with pride. "Olsen called on us while you was still out for the count, Captain. First day here. I made it known we wasn't gonna be soft shit in his hands like the rest of the guys in this pigpen." He shrugged. "I dunno, Captain. I guess a place like this needs an Olsen. Long as all the prisoners go along with the idea. Maybe the fat slob tried to stir up trouble for us on account of us tossin'

95

him out on his butt. And maybe the Rebs figured it'd be easier if there was two Olsens. Competition, like. Why? What's on your mind?"

"That woman."

Seward giggled. "You figure you're strong enough to do more than have her on your mind, Mr. Hedges?"

"Billy?" Forrest said evenly.

"Yeah, Frank?"

"How come you can get your rocks off when you ain't got the brains you was born with?"

"Uh, Frank?"

"He means your mind is between your legs, idiot!" Rhett rasped.

Seward scowled, then grinned as he thought of a retort. "So it gets wet every time I take a leak, Bob. Don't get dirtied up when I crap."

"Shut your friggin' mouths, all of you!" Forrest snarled. Then, to Hedges, "You figure she's a plant? What for?"

"You say she does some talking whenever she comes back from being cleaned up, Sergeant. Why not ask her?"

Silence descended over the men in their cramped, stinking quarters, as the troopers pondered the doubt which had been raised over the presence of Rose Walters. After a few minutes, Seward made to pose a question, but was driven back into silence by a glower from Forrest. Later, Rhett pointed out:

"If she is a Rebel spy, what could she possibly discover from us and the rest of the guys in this place?"

"Mouth, Rhett," Forrest said.

"Pardon, Sarge?"

"Only one we want to hear workin' is the woman's."

There was no further talk until supper time, and that was confined to sour-voiced complaints about the food.

Since he was now conscious and able to feed himself, Hedges received no preferential treatment and ate the same prison fare as the rest of the captives.

"Shit, ain't it, Captain?" Seward muttered when the meal was finished.

"Figure you'd recognize the taste, trooper," Hedges answered. "Way you have to keep on eating your words."

The putdown drew some smiles and a curt laugh from Rhett. Then followed another period of silence, as evening gave way to night and the sounds of activity throughout the whole of Andersonville dropped in volume. Nobody made a move to light the lamp which Forrest had taken from Olsen for no payment on the first day Hedges and his men entered the prison.

"They're bringin' her back," Douglas announced as a din of half-hearted whistles, ribald catcalls and cheers sounded outside.

"How you going to make her say what you want to hear, sir?" Bob Rhett asked, in keen anticipation of being a witness to suffering.

"Maybe I'll go for her pride, trooper," Hedges replied. "Tell her that if she doesn't talk, she'll lose her job to you."

Rhett scowled through the darkness at this latest taunt, but only Seward giggled at the New Englander's discomfort. The tramping footfalls of the prison guards came to a halt in front of the shebang.

"Wake up, you bluebellies," one of the Rebels snarled. "Compliments of Captain Wirz, your dreams have come true again."

The woman's head was tilted forward and she was given a vicious shove in the back. She groaned as she staggered inside, then gasped with shock as a man's arm encircled her waist, forcing her to an unexpected halt.

Outside in the moon-silvered Georgia night, the guards laughed and swaggered away toward the north gate. As Rose Walters' vocal response to shock was curtailed—trapped in her throat with her venting breath by a hand clapped over her mouth and nostrils.

Holding her tight against him, Hedges grimaced, feeling suddenly as weak as a new-born foal from the exertion of getting to his feet and from the involuntary reaction to embracing a soft-skinned, slender-framed, clean-smelling woman whose no-longer-lank hair brushed against his sweating and bristled face.

"I'll whistle somethin' if you wanna dance, Captain," Frank Forrest growled.

And this time it was only Bob Rhett who guffawed. Then cried out in pain as the elbow of Hal Douglas jabbed him hard in the ribs.

"You have the choice, lady," Hedges forced out through clenched teeth, sweat oozing from every pore as he struggled to overcome his initial response to holding her. "You can die slowly or fast. First choice comes when I take my hand off your face. Scream and you'll wake up dying. Slow."

He removed his hand and the breath rattled out of her throat. Then she made a slightly louder noise as she sucked in fresh air—or what passed for fresh air in the reeking atmosphere of Andersonville.

"I . . . I don't understand," she forced out. "Aren't you the . . . the one who—?"

"Lived off your immoral earnings," Hedges cut in on her. "But times have changed. I'm well enough to start killing Rebels again. And you're first in line."

His voice was less thick now, as he spoke the threatening words through her hair into her right ear.

"I'm not a Confeder——" she started.

Hedges hit her backhanded across the mouth and then cut her scream in half with the palm, as he raised a knee behind her legs and forced her over it. He lowered her to the dirt floor and dropped into a crouch at her side. Then he took both hands away from her.

She sucked in her breath and held it, as the other six men in the shebang shuffled forward and adopted similar attitudes to the captain, totally encircling her.

"You're a Confederate, lady," Hedges said softly, looking across her rigid body at Forrest and miming the act of drawing a weapon from a neck pouch.

The sergeant nodded and produced the straight razor from his pants pocket.

The woman saw the blade glint in the low level of

moonlight which entered the shack and gaped her mouth wide.

"Hold her!" Hedges ordered, and fixed a vice-like grip over her throat as Scott and Bell clutched a wrist and elbow each and Seward and Douglas pinned her knees and ankles to the ground. Rhett did not touch her, but uttered a low sound of anticipation as Forrest used the razor to slice through the ropes which held the blanket in place.

"Don't scream until you're hurt," Hedges said, his voice soft and even again, as he released his hold on her throat and she made a retching sound in expelling her breath. "Then you won't be able to help it. But only you will hear it, lady. Inside your own head."

He showed her what he meant, taking hold of a filthy kerchief and holding it two handed a few inches above her mouth. Forrest flipped open the blanket to bare her pathetically thin body.

"Why are you doing this to me?" she asked, terror making her voice a rasping whisper. "What have I done?"

"You're a good actress, lady," Hedges answered. "But the best whores always are. Part of the job."

"Please, I don't know what you mean?" she moaned.

"But you let the real you show through earlier today, lady," the captain continued. "The mask of suffering slipped and for a second or so you were all ears, as the saying is."

He had to make an effort to keep watching her wide-eyed, terror-stricken face, to fight against the compulsion to let his gaze wander over her exposed body. Not from fear that the sight of her nudity might spark a fresh arousal of lust. Instead, to keep from feeling pity for her.

There was no doubt in his mind that he was right about Rose Walters, that she had been given to the prisoners to spy upon them. A task that as a woman she could accomplish far better than any Rebel soldier who might be infiltrated among the Union men. Because she was able to move from one group of captives to another at their will, be used and cast aside—ignored in the aftermath of lust, weak and humiliated, but capable of listening to the talk of the men. And every two days, when she was taken to the fort outside the pine trunk fence, she could report what she had heard.

So, he had no doubt of this. He was also certain of something else—that Rose Walters was one of the bravest women involved in the War Between the States. Which was why he avoided looking at her naked body, which from slender thighs to the thin shoulders above her small breasts carried countless marks of the suffering she had endured for a cause in which she believed. He found it much easier to shun compassion by concentrating his attention on her face, watching her terror expand with each word *he* spoke.

And he spoke for upwards of two minutes, concluding with:

"It's the only way to explain why you were given to us, lady. We tried to escape before we got here. And that feller Wirz who runs this place figured that making an example of me wasn't enough to stop my buddies here from trying again to abuse his brand of Southern hospitality.

"And I guess Wirz wasn't too bothered when the prisoners started sharing you around. Gave you the opportunity to listen in on what a lot more men were talking about. How many plans for escape have you told Captain Wirz about, lady? Apart from the snatch of talk you heard earlier today—and let your mask slip to show me you'd heard?"

"Smart figurin', Captain," Scott congratulated.

The woman, who had constantly moved her head from side to side in an unbroken gesture of desperate denial to every word of accusation leveled at her, now blurted, "No, it's not true. None of it's true. I'm on your side. It's your men who have . . . I swear it. I was reporting to General Grant about Confederate troop movements when I was captured and—"

Her voice ceased to be a hoarse whisper and began to get shriller. Hedges scowled and clamped the kerchief between her parted lips. She squeezed her eyes tight closed.

"Keep it down, lady," the captain hissed.

Then her eyes snapped open to their fullest extent. Her body became rigid. And a main artery stood out through the skin of her thin neck like a length of thick, dark cord.

"Atta boy, Frank!" Billy Seward said with brutal glee.

Now Hedges' narrowed eyes looked down at the woman's body. And saw that the heel of Forrest's right fist rested on the center of her belly. And that a thin trickle of blood came out from under his hand, oozing up from the deep wound into which the full length of the razor's blade was sunk.

Hedges was not aware he had eased the pressure of the kerchief across the woman's open mouth. Until, as he stared with ice-cold anger at the sergeant, he heard her gasp:

"You'll pay, you Yankee sonsofbi . . ."

Forrest's expression of anger—a match for that of the captain's—was suddenly displaced by a grin of pure evil as he swept his fist to the side to open a long, gaping wound from the woman's navel to her hirsute sex organ. And her threat was left unfinished, punctuated by the death rattle sighing in her throat.

"That tell you what you wanted to know, sir?" the sergeant asked through his clenched teeth, as he pulled the razor free of the blood torrenting flesh.

"You sure enough got her to open up, Sarge," Rhett gloated.

The sensation of the ice-cold anger draining out of Hedges was almost a physical one and as the final heel-taps went, the grinning face of Forrest seemed to blur. Again he had to make a great effort to struggle against a bodily demand.

There *had* been doubt in his mind about Rose Walters. He had told himself there was none as a salve to his conscience. What if her sympathies were with the Union and he discovered this new torture he was inflicting was not deserved? Throughout the war, even amid the degradation of Andersonville, he had been as one with his men and yet always endeavored to remain fractionally above the depths to which their brutality and evil lowered them. But if the woman's dying words had not incriminated her . . .

"What'll we do with the corpse?" Bob Rhett asked, suddenly anxious.

"We toss it in the Sweetwater and the dead wagon'll pick her up like it always picks up the dead," Douglas suggested.

"But Wirz might—" the New Englander started.

"He won't do nothin'," Forrest cut in. "That sneaky little bastard claimed she was Union and he ain't never stirred no shit when other prisoners got wasted in this pigpen. One less mouth to feed is how he's gotta pretend to look at it." He had never shifted his gaze off Hedges' face while he replied to Rhett's objection. Now he posed, "Wouldn't you say, sir?"

The captain was deep in thought, forcing his mind to work as he continued to fight the danger of a faint that threatened to claim his sickness-weakened frame. He thought about the woman's bravery. About whether she was a whore from some Atlanta bordello impressed into serving the cause, or maybe a once-decent woman who had suffered tragedy by Union action—was made embittered enough to volunteer for this terrible duty.

"What was that, Sergeant?"

A shake of the head. "It don't matter, sir. Me and the rest of the guys got took in bad by this dame. You did okay. Now you rest up some more and we'll take care of what's left to do."

Hedges nodded and crawled across to the pile of straw, stretched out gratefully on his back.

"In the creek with her, Frank?" Douglas asked.

"No. We got the razor. Handle it right, we can cut her up in bits and bury her all over this stinkin' pigpen. Maybe get a charge some time seein' what the Rebs'll do if a chunk of her gets dug up."

"Hell, that's a lot of friggin' trouble to go to," Billy

Seward complained. "I'm for Hal's idea. Dump her in the creek. What do you say, sir?"

"Goodnight to you fellers," Hedges murmured. "To the lady, rest in pieces."

Chapter Four

EDGE and the widow of Jack Cash reached Pueblo San Luis at nightfall. They had seen the cluster of white adobe buildings from a long way off in the late afternoon, then lost sight of them behind a series of rises in the Sierra Madre foothills. They heard guitar and harmonica music from the village as the sun slid to a red death behind the western ridges. And when full night came to the mountains, lights gleamed a perhaps false welcome from windows a half mile distant.

The woman, whose only similarity to Rose Walters was that she had been ill-used by men, had told the half-breed the name of the village when it first came in sight.

"We got married there, Mr. Edge," she added, anxious to start a conversation which the man had constantly refused to do since they rode away from Flecha Mesa, leaving the corpses where they lay but taking the spare mounts on lead lines.

"Uh uh," he answered. "If it was in haste, you didn't have too much leisure to repent."

"Too long," she rapped. Then, hurrying to keep the exchange going, "Not just this morning. Couple of weeks ago, give or take a day. When Jack and Clyde stopped over on their way south. I'd been stuck there three weeks already after the sonofabitch who brought me to Mexico run out on me. I was outta money and patience and them two was a long time without female company. Jack kinda staked a claim on me while Clyde made time with the Mex whores."

"Mexican, lady."

"What?"

"Mexican whores. I'm half Mexican. You don't say the whole word, it sounds near as bad as greaser."

"Sorry."

"No need, long as you remember."

She expressed a grimace he did not see. Then continued, "Jack got drunk. I mean real, stinkin', blind drunk. On account of he was sick and tired of chasin' this fugative from San Antone for so long. But he acted like a gentleman, far as a gentleman can be that in this kinda back-of-beyond country. Didn't lay a finger on me. I figured him for an easy touch but when I asked him to stake me he turned me down flat. But said if I married him, I wouldn't ever have money worries again."

She shrugged. "So I figured, what the hell? Whoever heard of a bounty hunter that lived to a ripe old age? He didn't seem no worse than any other guy who'd got me with big promises. So I let him wake up the preacher in San Luis and we tied the knot. Mister, was that a mistake."

"You ain't the first that's made one of that kind," Edge offered as he lit a freshly rolled cigarette.

"First thing I find out, Jack was . . . what do you call it? He couldn't screw. He wanted to, but he couldn't. Sounds like important, but it sure ain't that."

"Impotent," Edge told her.

"Yeah, that's it. Real touchy about it, he was. Said he'd kill me if I ever let on. Until me, only Clyde Bodelle and Jack himself knew about it. I wasn't too damn happy about it at first, I can tell you. I get natural urges like normal folks and I ain't . . . im–pot–ent. But then I figured, what the hell? If Jack didn't get blasted by some outlaw him and Clyde was after, then I'd just up and leave the sonofabitch soon as I was some place back in the good old US of A."

"He got blasted, lady," Edge pointed out. "And you're headed in the wrong direction. Back to where it started."

"I got my reasons for comin' back to San Luis, Mr. Edge."

She eyed the half-breed as if she expected him to query this, but he said nothing and continued to smoke and survey his surroundings.

She shrugged and grimaced both. "Maybe it was on account of he couldn't get it up for a woman. Whatever, he liked slappin' them around. He sure lammed into me a few times while we tried to catch up on this guy from San Antone. And Clyde told me there had been other women. Whores, mostly. He used to pay big money to them if they let him beat up on them."

"It happens."

"But it seems I was special. You heard and saw the way he was back at Flecha Mesa. I was his lousy property and he didn't have to pay me a cent to knock me around. All he needed was an excuse. And he always got a bigger charge outta it when he figured I was makin' up to a man or let a man make up to me."

She laughed suddenly, throwing her head back and directing the harsh sound toward the darkening skies. "Brother, did I get that to backfire on the bastard today.

"They catch him?" Edge asked after a long silence which followed her joyful boast.

"What?"

"The feller from San Antone?"

"Hell, no. Guess that's what made Jack Cash more touchy than usual. They lost his trail down near Mesa del Huracan. Reason I know where that is. The place you're headed for."

The half-breed made to touch the shirt pocket with the letter in it, an unconscious gesture which he suddenly became aware of, and chose to scratch the lobe of an ear instead.

There was another long silence between them, until they heard the distant strains of Mexican music as the sun began to set. A mournful melody, like the musicians were regretting that the day was at an end.

"I guess you think of me as not much better than a

106

whore, mister?" she said, her tone a match for the melancholic music drifting through the barren hills.

"I don't think of you at all, lady."

Her green eyes flared with anger but when she peered through the twilight at his impassive profile she realized that the venting of such an emotion would merely relieve her of some pent-up tension—and not touch him at all.

"I think you're as hard as they come, mister," she accused, her tone emphatic but not loud.

"I am what I am. You're what you are. We just happen to be riding the same trail at the same time."

"Brother, did I read you wrong."

"I ain't changed since Flecha Mesa."

"And neither have I. I wasn't a whore then and I ain't one now. I never have been. I'm just a girl who never had any breaks. Make a habit of pickin' the wrong men. I try, believe me, I try. But it always happens they use me and leave me high and dry or they turn out to be sonsofbitches I have to get rid of."

Edge looked at her now, bristled face expressionless but curiosity in the way his head was cocked slightly to one side.

She showed him a brief smile, then shrugged her shoulders. "Yeah, mister. I figured that with you, my luck might change."

He looked away from her and spat a globule of saliva into the dust on the other side of the stallion. As they rounded a curve where the trail snaked through a fold in the hills and the lights of Pueblo San Luis showed through the darkness of full night.

"Yeah, real crazy, wasn't I?" Flo Cash admitted as the music, briefly curtailed, began again. Something lively now. "But what else was I to do? If you hadn't been around back there, I wouldn't have stirred up Jack. I liked your looks and the way you handled Jack. Figured you wouldn't let me down and you didn't. Far is it goes."

"It ain't gone anywhere, lady."

Another shrug of her shoulders. "So the hell with it.

107

Least you ain't done me no harm. I figure nine outta ten of the kinda men who ride this country wouldn't have let me keep my horse and ride with them. Not unless I paid them. In the only kinda way a destitute woman got to pay."

"You ain't just talking because you don't like the music," he said.

"Least I read you right there. But the best kinda man needs a woman from time to time. I ain't no ravin' beauty, don't I know that. I ain't so hard to look at, though. And I figured that after you'd allowed me to ride with you, well . . . maybe it wouldn't matter that we got off on the wrong foot."

"And now you've got no reasons for coming back here," Edge answered as they started up the gentle slope of a rise on the flat top of which the village was sited.

She showed another smile and through it vented a low sigh of resignation. "I tried and I lost out again, mister. Least this time I ain't got any scars to show for it. Except for a little damage to my pride. But if I hang around the cantina long enough, some guy is sure to come by to heal that."

The cantina, which was labeled by a sign for what it was without any distinctive name, was the largest of the single storey buildings in San Luis. It stretched the length of one side of the plaza which the trail entered from the north and left at the south-east corner.

Across from the cantina was a bank and a gunsmith' store. The newcomers rode onto the plaza between a small *Federale* post and a blacksmith forge. Opposite these was a livery stable and a grocery store. There was a wooden stoop in front of each building except the livery. At the center of the plaza was a clump of mesquite with some barrels encircling it to serve as seats.

Like Paraiso across the border to the north, Pueblo San Luis obviously existed for no other purpose than to serve the needs of transient outlaws and bounty hunters. But unlike in the American town, law and order was established here, the presence of the *Federale* post

108

signaling that whatever greeds and animosities existed out in the Sierra Madres, the village was a truce area.

"Just need my own horse and what's on him." Edge said as he dismounted in front of the livery which, like all the buildings except for the cantina and the *Federale* post, was in darkness. "Maybe you can sell what's left."

"Appreciate that," she answered. "No good bangin' on the door, mister. Paco'll be in the cantina. We leave them here, he'll come take care of them."

She slid wearily out of her saddle and looked around the plaza with distaste as they headed for the cantina.

"Paco'll buy the horses and saddles and stuff. Get enough for them to stake me for a long time in this hick town. Long enough maybe for ten men to ride through. You think that if I keep count and pick the tenth one, I could get it right this time?"

She laughed.

And he showed a smile with a hint of warmth along the mouthline. "Maybe. If you don't get tired of single-bed sleeping before your money runs out."

"Right, mister, right."

"No, lady. For you, I ain't Mr. Right."

She scowled, but only for a moment. Then, eagerly, "That proves I ain't a whore, though, don't it? For that kind, it's a job of work just for money. For me, it's fun."

He held open one of the batwing doors and she swept into the cantina, a hand raised in greeting and a broad smile on her flesh-thickening features.

"Hi, fellers! Like the bad penny, here I am turned up again!"

There were a dozen men and three women already in the cantina. All of them responded with matching warmth to her greeting, then eyed the tall, lean stranger with curiosity as he surveyed them and their surroundings.

One of the men was an American. A bald-headed old-timer of about seventy with a curly red beard arched along the line of his jaw. He sat alone at a table

109

sipping beer from a near empty glass and playing solitaire.

The musicians sat at a table at the far end of the bar which ran along the rear wall of the place. The bartender was behind his counter and the other eight men were split into two groups, playing cards for no stakes unless they took the form of drinks.

Except for the *Federale* sergeant, who was in his thirties, all the Mexican men were of late middle-age. The three thirty-or-so-year-old whores shared a table and bottle of tequila next to where the guitar and harmonica players were seated.

This left a lot of seating capacity free, which showed that business was slow in the cantina, and explained the eager smiles which were directed at Edge by the whores and the bartender as he crossed to a midway point in the counter. As Flo Cash engaged in earnest conversation with a paunchy player in the same card game as the *Federale*.

"*Señor,* your pleasure?" the beaming, fleshy-faced, thickly moustached bartender offered.

"Beer to start, feller."

"And what to follow, *hombre?*" the slimmest and most attractive whore called and clicked her fingers.

The musicians received the signal and switched to a soft and romantic tune.

"No chance, Maria," the American woman put in as she sat down at the whores' table, the man she had spoken to rose from his and the bartender placed a glass of foaming beer in front of the half-breed." Mr. Edge has somethin' on his mind that don't allow no room for women."

The whore muttered low words in Spanish, which cast doubt on the newcomer's manhood—attributing his condition to the fact that he was a *gringo*.

"I speak Spanish better than my Mexican father, lady," he answered in her language as the man who had left the card game halted beside him.

Maria poured and quickly drank two fingers of tequila.

110

"*Señor,* I am Paco," the paunchy Mexican announced, in English. "My livery, it is good. Flo, she say you can pay? I can believe her?"

Edge was careful not to reveal the size of his bankroll as he drew a ten-dollar bill from his pocket. "Can you believe this, feller?"

Paco grinned. "Your horse, I take good care of him, *señor.* How much time you stay here?"

"Tonight, tomorrow and tomorrow night," the oldtimer with the red beard put in, and nodded, blankfaced, when the half-breed looked at him. "Only take you three days to reach Mesa del Huracan crossin' the kind of country in the kind of weather that's between here and there. And you'll be more comfortable stayin' here in San Luis than killin' time down there."

"Tonight, at least, feller," Edge told Paco, as he picked up his beer, carried it to where the old man sat and dropped into the chair opposite him.

"Name's Howie Green, Mr. Edge. I heard that Flo gal call you that. Reason I knew you were headed for Mesa del Huracan."

The shadow of a man, cast by the two kerosene lamps hung from the ceiling, fell across the table. Edge looked up into the bristled, good-looking face of the *Federale* sergeant. The half-breed was aware that the man had gone to peer out over the tops of the batwing doors while Paco was talking to him.

"Sergeant?" he asked.

"It seems to me, *señor,* that the horses in front of Paco's place—two of them had other riders this morning."

"That's right."

"It happened far from this place, *señor?*"

"A man can ride a lot of miles from noon until now. Even through an afternoon as hot as this one was."

"*Si señor,*" He touched the peak of his cap. "But if I receive a complaint, I must act upon it."

Edge nodded, and Howie Green grinned as the *Federale* turned and went back to his card game.

"Reckon there won't be no complaints unless they be

111

from the woman and she ain't about to whine, eh?" the old-timer said in a rasping whisper. "On account of Cash and Bodelle wouldn't lose their horses unless they lost somethin' else first. Reckon they're dead out there someplace, eh? Buzzard meat. Corpses."

The half-breed took a first sip at his beer. "Remains to be seen, feller."

The grin expanded to a cackling laugh. And one booted foot thudded up and down against the floor. "Hey, I like that, mister. Remains to be seen. I like that."

"I don't like you haven't explained how you know about me and where I'm headed, feller," Edge said evenly as the smoke-layered, liquor-smelling cantina became as settled as it was before the newcomers entered.

It was a place where troublemakers came, and were welcome if they did not make trouble here. The kind of place where questions were never asked of strangers, who came only to be served with what San Luis supplied. There were the rules and if everyone complied with them, peace reigned. In the music-filled peace tonight, only Howie Green was close enough to this stranger to recognize that he was the kind to break every rule there was, if that was what it took to get what he wanted.

The old-timer took a swallow at his beer to empty the glass, licked his thin lips and blinked his dark eyes several times. "Now, Mr. Edge, you got no call to talk tough to me. I'm the gunsmith around here. I don't need no dollar handouts to deliver messages."

"So deliver it for free, feller."

"Intend to, mister. It was one of the Murphy brothers give me the buck. Give that to the priest that runs the church over the hill. To put in the poor box. You wanna donate, I'll be happy—"

"Make me happy, feller."

"Eh? Oh, yeah. Last night Pat Murphy come to San Luis. To buy groceries and some shells. Said a feller name of Edge would likely ride through here. Said to tell you him and his brother Sean still got what you want. And the time and the day ain't changed."

"That all?"

"Sure enough is."

"Who are the Murphy brothers?"

The wrinkle-skinned face was contorted by a grimace and Green spat at the floor. "A couple of no-account bounty hunters. Been ridin' up and down this trail for these past five years at least. Pickin' up the leavin's of other men. The poor bastards that are only worth twenty-five or maybe fifty bucks to the law north of the border. Yellow-backed little bastards who ain't got the spunk to go after killers and bank robbers and the real mean hold-up men."

"Obliged," Edge said. "You want another dollar for the poor box? Or a drink?"

There was relish in the way the old man licked his lips this time. "I'll take the drink, mister. I got my suspicions that money is apt to drop outta the priest's poor box and into his pocket."

Edge nodded, turned to locate the bartender and called, "Bottle of rye and two shot glasses, feller."

The order was delivered to the table just as Paco returned to the cantina and announced:

"Horses all bedded down fine, *señor*."

"Obliged." He filled both glasses to the brim and said as he lifted one to his lips, "Three-day ride, uh?"

Green nodded. "That's right, mister. Gives you two nights and a day in hand. Luck to you."

He tossed back his drink at a swallow.

"You figure I'll need it? Against the Murphies?"

"Well . . . " He reached for the bottle, looked at Edge and did not pour himself a drink until he received a nod. "Well, like I told you, they're yellow. But I been around in this world seventy years I know about, mister. And on the whole, men that ain't got no spunk, they're apt to be real sneaky bastards. And I've heard tell that the Murphy brothers are two of the slyest little sonsofbitches that ever grew to be five feet tall." He vented another cackling laugh. "It's said they never

113

grew full size on account it was so long before somebody lifted the rock so they could crawl out from under
it!"

"*Señor?*"

Edge turned in his chair to look at the bartender.

"*Señora* Cash, she wishes for my wife to cook her
something to eat. It will be no trouble to cook extra."

"Obliged. You have rooms here?"

"*Si señor.*"

"Fine."

"You wish for a single or a double room, *señor?*"

"A double, feller. But only because I like to stretch
myself out."

"Very well. But if you should change your mind,
señor, Maria, Juanita and Margarita are all guaranteed
to satisfy."

"If your food's as good as your liquor, I'll be satisfied, feller."

The three whores scowled their disapproval of the
outcome of the exchange. The American woman who
shared their table showed a quiet smile.

"Do something for me, Howie?" Edge asked.

"What I can."

"In a while I'm going to eat. After that, do some
drinking. If I start to act like I'm taking a fancy to any
of those women over there, you take the bottle away
from me, uh?"

"An old man like me take somethin' away from
you?" Green answered incredulously.

"If you need to. I'll be real drunk, feller. Ain't been
drunk often. Whenever it happened, I was never any
trouble to anyone."

Green looked like he did not believe this. But he
sighed and nodded. "All right if I take a drink every
now and then."

"Sure thing."

"Somethin' else, mister."

"What's that?"

"Like to ride out to the old *Federale* post at Mesa

114

del Huracan with you. Do this old body of mine a power of good to see the Murphies get what's comin' to them."

"It ain't exactly the Murphies I'm after, feller."

A shake of the head. "That don't matter, mister. Them pint-size bastards don't ever deal straight. They'll try to cheat you, some way or other. Can't help it. It's in their nature. And I figure you ain't the kinda man takes easy to gettin' cheated."

They had two more shots of whiskey each, then the food arrived; a plate heaped with enchiladas and a bowl of chili on the side. It was good, hot and filling and the bartender beamed at the obvious relish with which the stranger ate the meal and continued to show his appreciation of a free spending customer after the half-breed called for a fresh bottle of rye whiskey.

Edge had spoken the truth when he told Howie Green he did not often get drunk. The last time had been in San Francisco, a unique occasion since he had mixed heavy drinking with a high-stakes poker game. The time before that was when . . .

He closed his mind to memories of that other unique occasion. And he also refused to consider the reason why he had elected to get drunk tonight. Instead, he reflected upon the circumstances of his surroundings which made it safe for him to abandon his normal attitude of watchfulness.

These were surroundings in which no threat of danger lurked so long as a man could pay for what he had, which meant that the presence of the *Federale* sergeant was superfluous in the maintenance of law and order. For the requirements of travelers and the ability of the merchants of Pueblo San Luis to supply their needs was almost by itself a guarantee that the tiny village remained peaceful. And the seal was set on the guarantee by the nature of the men who needed what it supplied.

Desperate men or those with a singlemindedness of purpose, for no one rode lightly into the Sierra Madre. All of them hard because they had to be that to ride the

115

harsh country which surrounded the village. Some of them brutal. Some downright evil. But in certain respects they were like all men.

They got hungry and they got a thirst for more than mere water. On occasions they needed somewhere safe to put their money, a haven to rest up without fear of attack, a place to have their horses shod, a place to get fresh supplies of food and shells, a place to buy a willing woman, and maybe sometimes, a man needed the church over the hill to pray at.

Whatever it was such men wanted, they were the kind who got it—or were vicious in their disappointment. So anyone who caused trouble in Pueblo San Luis —damaged its reputation as a safe area amid a petrified ocean of danger—would be a fool of the first order, living on borrowed time with countless guns seeking to call in the loan.

For a few moments, shortly after he entered the cantina, Edge might well have become such a fool—in his initial response to Howie Green's knowledge of his destination.

But he had got over that hurdle. He grinned at the red-bearded old-timer and then showed the expression to the rest of the music, talk and smoke-filled room. Howie, right across the table from him, was in sharp focus. But everyone else looked a little blurred. Including the tall, thin man who came in through the batwing doors.

Edge nodded and grunted and Green asked him what he had said. But the half-breed kept his thoughts to himself. He had got over one hell of a lot of hurdles in his life to survive as long as he had done, due largely to his habitual alertness. But he did not need to maintain a constant watch on his surroundings tonight and it was good to relax, good to know that the people of Pueblo San Luis meant him no harm. Any stranger who might ride out of the Sierra Madre into the village would know the rules—or quickly learn them.

A stranger had come in. He remembered seeing him

push open the batwings. He turned on his chair to look for him. But could not see him.

He couldn't see Flo either. The three whores were still at the table beside that where the musicians were playing. But the American woman who was so insistent that she was not a whore had left.

Even in his liquor-sodden mind, he was surprised at his response to her absence. She was right. She wasn't a whore, just a woman who for some reason had found herself out on the frontier; a man's land. And she had survived with dignity, in her view, passing from one no-good drifter to the next but never selling herself the way Maria, Juanita and Margarita did. Marrying just one of her partners, but convinced that she was as good as other women who took and lost a string of husbands.

"Where she go?" Edge asked Green, aware of the slur in his voice.

"Who, mister?"

"The woman I came in with?"

Green's frown of anxiety deepened. "Out to one of the back rooms. With the guy that fetched her here in the first place. Then run out on her. He come back."

The half-breed felt himself plumb the depths of drunken depression. "She didn't deserve the way I treated her."

"What?"

"I was a real sonofabitch to her."

Green looked away from the bristled face of Edge. "Well, you got time to say you're sorry, mister. If you've a mind."

Edge, swaying on his chair and spilling rye from the glass in his hand, turned to gaze in the same direction as Green. And saw the woman coming along the bar. She wore a dress now. White, low at the neckline, tight to her torso and falling full from the waist. She had taken a bath and washed and combed her hair, powdered and painted her face. With the skill of her sex, she had succeeded in emphasizing her most attractive features, and Edge had the presence of mind to wonder

117

if, had he not been drunk, she would still have looked radiantly beautiful to him.

The tall, thin, handsome young man who had earlier entered the cantina, halted a couple of feet behind her when she stopped at the half-breed's table. He wore a suit, shirt, string tie and vest and carried a Stetson.

"Vic came back for me, Mr. Edge," the woman said, smiling. "He went all the way down to Mazatlan and look what he bought me."

She held out her arms to the side and half-turned, one way and then the other.

"You look fine," Edge told her, uncomfortably aware that he was stirred by the sight of her, the smell of her and the way the skirts of her dress rustled as she moved.

"We're leavin' now. Right now. Tonight. Aimin' for San Francisco."

"That's fine," Edge said.

Vic moved up beside the woman. "Flo told me about what happened, mister. I want to thank you for taking care of her the way you did."

"I didn't do anything, son." He heard the slur in his voice, but guessed he had managed to keep the bitterness of disappointment hidden.

"I want to thank you, too." She bent down to him as she spoke, and her perfume was strong in his nostrils as her lips brushed his bristled cheek. "Goodbye, Mr. Edge."

Vic took hold of her arm and they headed for the batwings, responding to a chorus of goodbyes from the Mexicans. Edge watched them until they went from sight into the darkness of the plaza.

"Maybe he'll turn out to be one in ten."

"Uh?" Howard Green grunted.

"Nothing, feller." The half-breed grinned, drank what had not been spilled from his glass and poured another. Then pushed the bottle toward the old timer. "Here, you can start matching me drink for drink now."

118

"Appreciate it, mister," Green said, tipping the bottle above his glass.

Edge nodded. "Yeah, appreciation is what it's all about, feller." He raised his glass in a toast. "To Vic. Who just relieved me of a Flo Cash problem."

The Drunk

At the close of Sioux Uprising, *Edge discovers that his
wife is dead, had died in such a way that he was com-
pelled to share in the blame for the tragedy. In the
opening chapter of the next book in the series—*The
Biggest Bounty—*he rides through the emptiness of
northern Wyoming Territory, attempting to come to
terms with what has happened. There is a reference to
him stopping off in only one town during his long and
lonely ride, to replenish his supplies. "He had wasted
little time in making the purchases and ridden out fast,
veering away from the trail to ensure that he continued
to suffer the bitter pangs of grief in isolation." Actually,
he had time enough to get drunk enough to forget that
what follows happened.*

EDGE rode into town from the east at a time in the
afternoon when it should still have been quite light.
But the low cloud and the rain it poured down upon the
foothills of the Wyoming Rockies created the conditions
of late evening. So that he was not aware that a town
was nearby until he was flanked by buildings instead of
prairie as the trail became a street.

And for several moments he thought it was a ghost
town. For there were no lights at any windows he could
see and, as he angled his gray gelding into the lee of the
buildings along the windward side of the street, he saw
that few of the windows had glass in them.

The half-breed pursed his lips and vented a low sigh
of resignation to adversity as he rode by the end of a

120

row of houses and started across the front of some business premises. Stores, a bank, a newspaper, land and lawyer's office, the painted lettering on their shingles just discernible—the façades to which the shingles were fixed in as bad a state of repair as the houses back along the street.

When the gelding snorted, the rider misunderstood the reason for the equine response and ran a hand gently down the side of the animal's neck.

"Never does rain but it pours, does it feller," he said softly. "Look on the bright side, though. Plenty of water and lots of places to get in out of the wet. For free."

Nothing about the demeanor of the tall, lean, blue-eyed, black-haired stranger to town suggested he felt like looking on the bright side of anything. And the expression on his heavily bristled face did not alter when he reached a section of street where lights did gleam from some windows, he smelled smoke in the rain needled air, and the horse snorted again—scenting its own kind in the vicinity.

There was a livery stable here, a saloon, an office building with several shingles flanking the door, and a few stores supplying the basic necessities of frontier life. These occupied premises, frame-built and all two storeys high, were less neglected than those which had been abandoned—and those along the street west of the mid-town area which he could see in the lamplight were also derelict—but it was apparent that only the most essential repair chores had been done. No work had been undertaken for purely cosmetic purposes.

As he dismounted in front of the saloon, the sign above the door naming the community as Mayville, the half-breed realized that even in the best of circumstances the place would be unprepossessing. Under assault by heavy rain driven by a forceful norther this town huddled on the south-east bank of the rushing Greybull River looked forbiddingly grim.

Like Edge himself did to the three people already in the saloon, as he pushed open the one-piece door and stepped inside, rain dripping off the brim of his Stetson and the bottom of the slicker caped over his shoulders.

"Sure is filthy weather, ain't it mister?" the short, thin, crafty-eyed man behind the bar counter greeted. "Shot of somethin' to get the chill outta your bones?"

"Obliged."

The saloon was big, but most of it was in darkness. Just two of the many ceiling-hung kerosene lamps were lit, dropping cones of yellow on to the center section of the long counter at the rear of the room and a half dozen chair-ringed tables immediately in front of it. The place smelled of cigar smoke, damp, dust, decay and dereliction.

As Edge started into the patch of light and across it, the fifty-year-old bartender set down a glass and filled it with whiskey, grinning his pleasure at doing business. And a man and a woman sharing a table eyed the newcomer appraisingly—like they were trying to figure out if he was a suitable customer for whatever they had to sell.

"Which way are you headed, sir?" the man asked. He was about fifty. Five-foot-six tall and a lot of pounds overweight—the blubber evenly distributed over his thighs, belly, chest, shoulders and face. He was dressed in a threadbare suit that had once been stylish and rested one of his feet on a valise at the side of his chair.

"West," Edge answered as he placed a dollar on the countertop and swallowed the rye before the bartender made change.

"Shit," the man said.

The woman laughed. It was a pleasant sound, vented from a pleasant face. She was a dyed blonde in her late twenties, about five-foot-three-inches tall and with a good shape. The frill-trimmed red-and-white gown she wore was designed to show off her curves to the best advantage and she knew how to apply paint and powder to emphasize her most attractive features. There was no doubt about what she had to sell.

"My answer or your feelings about it, feller?" Edge

122

asked coldly after he nodded to the bartender for a refill and turned to look at the fat, suit-attired man.

"Uh?" the man was suddenly nervous, frightened by the chill in the slitted blue eyes which gazed fixedly into his face. He shook his head vigorously, flabby cheeks quivering. "I assure you I wasn't implying anything about you, sir," he said quickly. "I intend to travel east. But I'm not exactly well-fitted for riding this country alone. I was hoping you would be—"

"West is the way I'm heading," Edge cut in and turned to the bar again, to raise the fresh drink. He sipped at it this time, intent on making it his last but reluctant to be done with the warmth which the liquor was spreading through his body. "After I've bought some supplies for the trail."

His stubbled, cold-pinched, rain-run face asked a tacit question of the bartender.

"Grocery store'll be open for another hour, mister. Or Fred'll open up any time if you got money to spend."

"Like you, George," the whore said, her good humor gone. "And any other business in this stinkin' town."

Now the fat man at her table laughed at her. "But there isn't a single enterprise in Mayville that is open longer than your legs, Belle."

"Or wider, Mr. Winters," George added, and showed just a few rotten teeth in otherwise puckered gums as he grinned.

"Ha, ha," the whore said, and it announced a vocal silence in the saloon.

Rain beat at the roof and walls and the logs on a stove in a darkened area crackled and spat as droplets of water found their way down the smoke stack.

"You come far, mister?" Belle asked at length, her tone bored.

"I come from way back, lady," he replied.

"Not so long," she answered. "I reckon you're the youngest and the most man that's been in this lousy town since the anthrax hit."

123

Edge half-turned to lean a hip against the bar front. "Did you say anthrax, lady?"

"No problem to you or your mount, mister," George said dully, as unhappy as Winters and the whore now that it seemed the half-breed was not going to buy any more drinks. "It happened three years ago."

"But Mayville never recovered from it," Winters added, shaking his head. "Town had a population of two hundred and fifty in its heyday. Plus another hundred or so folk living out on the ranches around here. The disease wiped out every single animal those ranches ran. Few people bought new stock and started up again. Not enough to support a town the size of Mayville, though."

"Mr. Winters run the Mayville Advocate," George said. "Finally had to close down the paper."

"Circulation of fifty copies a week isn't exactly economic, sir," the newspaperman muttered.

"And ain't one of them fifty people who bought the paper ever did any damn thing worth writin' in the paper about," the whore growled.

Edge had been making a genuine effort to be interested in the story of the dying town. Knowing this aim was as doomed as Mayville. But the experiment was worthwhile. Anything which might conceivably help him overcome, even for a few minutes, his depthless grief about the death of his wife demanded to be tried.

When he turned his back on the couple at the table again and fisted a hand around the shot glass, he saw that it was empty.

"Another, mister?" George asked eagerly, reaching down the bottle from a shelf.

Anything? Liquor would do it. If he could get drunk enough, the mental image of Beth's dead face which he had carried away from the small Dakotas farmstead would certainly become blurred by alcohol and then blotted out completely by the merciful darkness of drunken stupor.

As he rode the long miles westward, he had always been aware of alcohol as an answer to what ailed him.

124

And it was largely because of this temptation that he had stayed clear of towns until he rode by accident into Mayville. This was not the sole reason, for towns meant people, and the proximity of people had always threatened danger for the half-breed—since those opening days of the War Between the States when he came to realize what kind of cruel fate ruled his destiny.

But he had never been in greater danger than during the ride from the farm where Beth was buried to this grim Wyoming town. For by the cruelest twist of fate ever to torment him, he was made to feel responsible for the terrible way in which his wife died. And so it was not just grief that rode with him. There was also a powerful self-anger, a well of bitterness for his ruling fate and a mindless hatred for a world in which a man could be made to suffer such boundless anguish.

With his mind in such an emotional turmoil, Edge was aware that he would be unable to maintain the constant state of vigilance by which he had survived until now. Also, he knew that his unreasoning hatred for the world in general might well be channeled into and find outlet in an act of brutal violence against a fellow human being who meant him no harm.

He looked down at the glass in his fist and saw it was again filled with whiskey, raised his narrowed eyes and gazed into the thin face of the bartender. The man swallowed hard and took a staggering backward step, like he had been physically pushed by some palpable force emanated from the glittering slivers of icy blueness.

"What—?" he started to croak.

For just a part of a second the half-breed was on the point of streaking the hand away from the brimful glass, drawing the straight razor from his neck pouch and slashing at the scrawny throat of George. A man who meant him no harm. A man in the business of selling liquor who could not possibly know that he was luring his latest customer into the jaws of an inviting and obvious trap. These jaws liable to snap shut before the half-breed could escape.

That was the threat which was posed by the temptation of alcohol—the merciful relief of anguish, once
tried, could well prove too difficult to resist again. And
again.

"No sweat, feller," Edge said evenly, and felt the
skin of his face become less taut between the cheek and
jaw bones as he raised his glass to his lips. "I was thinking of somebody else."

George thrust out his lower lip and blew air up over
his sweating face. "Mister, I'm sure glad I ain't the one
you was thinkin' of when you looked at me that way."

"If you were, your troubles would be over."

He took half the drink at a swallow and in doing so
admitted defeat for the first time in his life. And already his mind felt easier. If being drunk proved too
appealing to ever be sober again, then maybe the liquor
would kill him. Or if his body refused to be poisoned,
then maybe one of his many enemies—or even a passing stranger in a mood as black as his own—might finish him quicker.

He was prepared to take the chance, which was a
measure of his desperation.

"Buy the bottle, feller?"

George showed both palms after setting the bottle
down. "Sure, mister. Be my guest."

"May need to be that." He took the bottle and glass
and sat down at the nearest table. "If it gets so I can't
handle a horse, I guess you got a room to rent?"

"Right."

"Horse hitched to your rail. You have anyone who'll
take him over to the livery?"

"I'll take care of it."

The bartender came out from behind his counter and
went to the door. Rain was blown across the threshold
as he went out.

"Not good for a man to drink alone, mister."

Edge finished his third rye and poured another before he looked across the intervening table to where
Winters and the whore sat. For the first time, he no-

ticed that they did not have drinks in front of them. It was the newspaperman who made the comment.

"If you buy the lady one as well, you won't be, feller."

Belle laughed.

Winters scowled. "I'm busted, mister."

"If money's all you're out of, you got nothing to complain about." He took this fourth drink at a single gulp. But was still able to see the maggots writhing between Beth's eaten away lips.

"Spare me your hard-luck story, mister," the fat man muttered.

Edge nodded as he poured another drink.

"You oughta get outta those wet clothes, mister," the whore with the pleasant looks advised.

It was the kind of thing Beth might have said. Edge shook his head and looked away from the whore, suddenly concerned about a side effect of his drinking which he had not considered before. What if the liquor did not serve its intended purpose? What if, when his brains were cooked in alcohol, he decided to try blotting out his pain by using the body of a woman? An available woman who was a whore? Hell, that would be like crapping on the new grave in which he had laid Beth to rest.

"Am I bothering you, lady?" he asked harshly. "Or you, mister?"

They said nothing, perhaps afraid that any word they spoke might harden the stranger's attitude even more.

He nodded. "So obliged if you'd do me the courtesy of not bothering me."

George returned to the saloon, seemed about to say something to the stranger, but kept silent when Belle looked hard at him and shook her head.

The half-breed continued to sit hunched at the table, his bristled, gaunt, weary-looking face set in an impassive cast. The only moves he made involved pouring fresh drinks and throwing them at the back of his throat. Behind the slitted eyes under their hooded lids, he allowed his mind to float free, making no efforts to

127

block from it the mental images of times—good and bad—during the tragically brief period he had known and loved Beth.

He was totally detached from his squalid surroundings of the decaying saloon in the dying town. New customers came in and left and he remained unaware of their pressence—of the way they directed surreptitious glances at him while they drank liquor or beer, heads bent across the bartop to listen to the whispered words of George. He did not even know when, or how many times, the bartender came to the table, took away an empty bottle and replaced it with a full one, uncapped and ready to be poured.

He thought about his first meeting with Elizabeth Day. She was naked, bathing her slim, high-breasted body in the rushing water of a stream.

About the way he had won the first battle toward making her his wife when he beat out Jonas Pike.

About their encounter with another newspaperman. Not named Winters. Named . . . Miles, that was it. Cyril Miles.

About how, not long after Miles died, Beth Day became Mrs. Josiah C. Hedges—married to a man who vainly hoped that by reverting to his former name and buying a farmstead in the Dakotas not too unlike the one he had inherited in Iowa, he could alter the course of his destiny.

About the Indian uprising that . . .

"Luck to you, Mr. Winters!"

The words, yelled close to his ear, triggered Edge out of his reverie. He jerked up his head and felt a damp wind blow into his face. Saw that the door of the saloon was open and a familiar figure stood there. The fat newspaperman, one hand on the door and the other clutching his valise. George stood beside the table, in process of switching a fresh bottle for an empty one.

The half-breed shot forward a hand and fisted it hard around the bartender's wrist. George was surprised enough to drop the full bottle of rye. It toppled on to its side, rolled across the table and shattered when it hit the floor.

"What's the matter, mister?" the man asked, voice shrill with fear.

"How many's that?"

The thin face blurred, looking like other indistinct faces the half-breed had been remembering.

"That's the fifth. I'll get another."

"Enough. I'm ready for that room now."

He released the wrist and looked around him. Winters was still on the threshold, letting cold, wet air into the stove-heated atmosphere of the saloon. Belle was where she always had been. But her lipstick was smudged and her hair was mussed. Like she had been entertaining a customer and did not expect another one tonight. There was nobody else in the saloon.

"Whatever you say, mister. I'll show you where it is."

"No, feller. She'll show me."

He pointed toward Belle. His arm wavered and his hand shook. He knew his voice was slurred.

The whore got to her feet, patting her disarrayed hair and frantically darting out her tongue to lick her lipstick.

"Be happy to, mister."

"Bye all," Winters called and closed the door behind him.

Edge got to his feet and knew it was not the room that tilted, instead, the illusion was caused by the swaying of his body. The whore ran to his side and fastened a grip on his arm.

"You need help, Belle?" George asked.

"When did I ever need help in handlin' a man?" she answered proudly.

The half-breed thought of something he wanted to say, but immediately forgot it. He had to concentrate all his mental ability on the physical chore of staying on his feet.

"This way, mister," Belle instructed, her grip firm but the pressure with which she guided him gentle. "Along to the end of the bar and up the stairs. You can

129

make it. There's a big, beautiful bed up there. The kind of bed where a man can forget whatever the hell it is that's troublin' him."

Edge felt weary and he felt sick. Out of the patch of light from the two kerosene lamps the shadowed area of the saloon appeared to him to be pitch black. Had he not had the whore as a guide, he would certainly have tumbled over the dusty furniture in an unused area of the big room.

Climbing the stairway threatened him with total exhaustion and he leaned heavily on Belle. So that she had to stop talking and devote all she had to keep from collapsing under his weight.

At the top she leaned him against a wall while she opened a door. Then steered him inside, turned him and lowered him to a bed.

He had been conscious of her perfume from time to time. As he sprawled out on his back, relishing the softness of the mattress beneath him, the scent was much stronger, and constant now.

"Reckon a two-buck quickie won't be any use to a man in your condition, mister," the whore said. "You'll need the five-dollar treatment. Or I'll stay all night, if you wanna pay ten."

"I'll pay ten, lady," Edge answered, opening his eyes as lamplight spread across the room from where she stood at a bureau.

"Money first, mister. You ain't paid George yet, except for the first few belts you had."

The bed smelled of her perfume. There were frilled curtains at the room's only window. A strip of rug on the floor, and some pen and ink sketches of cities on the walls. Otherwise it was like most other hotel rooms Edge had slept in. A bed, a chair and a bureau with a pitcher and basin for washing beside the kerosene lamp.

"I'm good for it," the half-breed muttered as he pulled himself up on the bed and leaned his shoulders against the headboard. Then reached down and began to take off his boots.

"I ain't doubtin' that, mister. But will I be able to get

what's owed after I've supplied what's needed? Here, I'll do that."

As she came away from the bureau, Edge was able to see his reflection in the mirror propped on it. The first time he had seen himself since . . . long before Beth died.

"Lady, I wouldn't trust a man who looked like me," he growled, frowning at the gauntness of his features, the hollowness of his eyes, the ingrained dirt in the exposed flesh and the irregular bristles which covered the rest of his face and throat. Then he hardened his tone as she stopped by the bed and stooped to tug at one of his mud-caked boots. "Leave it!"

"What?" she answered, stepping away from him, as frightened as George had been at the latent cruelty which was abruptly visible on the surface of his eyes.

"I never even let Beth take my clothes off, lady."

"Who?" Her pleasant looking features suddenly showed enlightenment. "Oh, it's a woman that's driven you to the bottle!"

At no time while he was drinking had Edge felt good. Ever since he felt the soft bed under his back, the effects of the liquor had gotten worse. There was a foul taste in his mouth, a nagging ache behind his eyes and a churning sensation in his stomach. Now, as he got off the first boot and lay back against the headboard again, the whore's perfume seemed suddenly much stronger in his nostrils and threatened to erupt nausea into his throat.

"Forget her, lady. That's what I'm trying to do."

"Pay me the ten and I'll do my damndest to help you."

"Twenty."

"Twenty?" She was both delighted by the offer and anxious about what she was required to do to earn it.

"Double to take care of your injured professional pride. On account of I don't want you to share this bed with me."

He got off the second boot and sighed his relief at the achievement.

131

"What then? What do you want me to do?"

"Wake me in four hours," he answered, taking off his hat and dropping it to the floor on his boots. Then he slid down to stretch out full length on the bed.

"Wake you? Hell, mister, you ain't gonna pay me twenty bucks just to do that."

"That's right. When I wake up, I want to have my horse saddled and ready to leave. I want the saddlebags to be packed with supplies and the canteens filled with fresh water. I want a couple of cartons of shells for my Winchester and I want a Colt .45 to put in my empty holster. Enough shells for the handgun to fill the loops of my gunbelt."

She was perplexed, then resigned, finally smiling with happiness. "Sure, mister. The customer's always right. And I ain't gonna ask you why doin' that is worth twenty bucks to you."

"Making sure I ain't going to do it is worth twenty, lady," he answered, closing his eyes against the lamplight.

Belle looked down at him for stretched seconds, head cocked to one side, frowning. Then she glanced over her shoulder at her reflection in the bureau mirror, at the revealing dress she wore and the damage which her last customer had done to her appearance.

"Guess Beth must have been quite a woman, mister," she said, soft and sad. "Liquor and whores ain't no use to you. Maybe driftin' out there away from people is the only thing that is."

Edge opened one eye as, almost lost behind her words and the drumming of the rain against the saloon, he heard the sound of a horse being ridden slowly along the muddy single street of Mayville.

"Sleep helps, lady," he said. "Obliged if you'd do like I ask."

"Be glad to. And I reckon I can trust you for the twenty, mister. But Fred over to the grocery store and Alvin at the livery only do cash business."

Edge nodded, rolled over on to his side and reached

a hand into the back pocket of his pants. Froze when his probing fingers failed to find the money they sought.

Suddenly, he felt stone-cold sober. And Belle took another backward step from the bed as she saw again the killer glint in the slits of his eyes.

"What's the matter?" she asked hoarsely.

Edge went over onto his back again, swung his legs to the side, pressed his bare feet to the floor and stood up. The room threatened to tilt, but he fought to maintain his balance.

"Can't be you, lady," he said, voice cold and hard. "Or you wouldn't have asked for money."

"You mean you've been—?"

"Robbed, lady." He sat down on the bed again and pulled on his boots. "And I seem to recall that only you and George got close enough to me to pick my pocket."

"George wouldn't have . . . Hey, wait a minute! Harry Winters. That fat slob went past your table on his way outta the saloon."

"Maybe some others, lady? Also seem to recall folks came and went while I was—"

"Sure. But they all stayed well clear of you, mister. On account George warned them you weren't in any mood to be bothered."

"Except by a feller who's busted and real eager to leave town. Put out the light, lady."

"What?"

"The light. Douse it!"

"Oh." She went to the bureau and turned down the wick of the kerosene lamp.

As Edge crossed to the window and tugged at the curtain so hard it fell to the side. There was a mist of condensation on the pane. Rain drops lashed in at his face when he jerked up the window with both hands and leaned out. The cold wetness of the rainstorm served to further diminish the effects of the alcohol coursing through his bloodstream.

"Mister, you can't be certain it was him!" Belle shrieked.

The newspaperman was on the center of the street immediately in front of the saloon. He reined his horse to a halt. Perhaps he heard the sound of the window being opened. Maybe the shrill words of the whore reached his ears. Or it could have been that he simply sensed a threat. Whichever, he turned in the saddle to look up at the rain-needled darkness above the saloon's lighted windows. And the half-breed saw terror inscribed into the soft flesh of the man's pudgy face, saw it too in Winters' rigid posture.

The half-breed ducked his head, swung a leg over the sill and stepped out onto the roof of the saloon's stoop.

Winters heard boot-leather on timber and jerked his head up. Then down, to see Edge drop in silhouette against a lighted window, hit the street in a splash of mud.

"You took my money!" the half-breed yelled, and lunged forward, the ankle-deep mud sucking at his feet.

The fat man gasped and his terror expanded to petrify him for a moment. Then he yelled at his mount and thudded his heels into its flanks.

The animal snorted and reared, alarmed by the sudden demand.

Winters screamed. In fear and at the horse.

Edge closed the gap and thudded his shoulder into the left hindquarter of the horse just as it was about to lunge into a gallop. At the same time as he fixed a double-handed grip on Winters' ankle.

The fat man's scream lengthened and became shriller. Doors were wrenched open as the horse powered forward, and Winters was dragged from his saddle. He and the man who had unseated him fell hard into the mud.

Voices were raised, demanding answers to questions. Belle's shrill words seemed not to be heard.

When Edge released his hold on Winters, the fat man tried desperately to crawl away. But he made it only a few feet through the clinging mud before Edge caught him, threw him onto his back and crouched down beside him—lowered the blade of the straight razor to his throat.

"Turns out you didn't take it, I'll stand you to a hot tub, feller," the half-breed rasped.

Figures loomed up out of the rain on either side of where one man held another helpless.

Rain beat down on Winters' fleshy face, washing off the mud. Tears welled in his eyes and spittle bubbled out over his quivering lips.

"Please," the fat man forced out.

"What's the friggin' idea, mister?" George snarled.

"Winters stole the stranger's bankroll," Belle said, breathless after a frantic dash down the stairs and out of the saloon.

"Wondered where he got the money to pay for what he bought off me," a man growled.

Winters was half-sunk in the mud but it was not this which prevented him from moving a muscle in his spreadeagled body and limbs as he stared up into the face of Edge.

"You gotta be crazy, Mr. Winters," George said. "Stealin' from a guy like this one."

The newspaperman tore his eyes away from the face of the half-breed and darted them back and forth along the sockets, searching for a sign of help. But if he was able to see anyone, no familiar features expressed anything that could hold his frantic gaze and he stared again into the impassive face of Edge.

"Please," he said again. "I needed the money bad. I could have rotted here in this town. I had to get away. You were drunk. I've never seen anyone drunker. I thought—"

"Where's the money, feller?"

"I spent twenty bucks, mister. At Fred's grocery store. The rest is in my inside jacket pocket."

Edge kept his right wrist on Winters' shoulder, the blade of the razor resting on the fleshy throat of the newspaperman, as he delved under the sodden jacket. He extracted a billfold, opened it one handed on Winters' chest and slid out the banknotes.

"You were flat broke before?"

"Yeah. Yes I was. If I hadn't been then I wouldn't—"

"Don't matter, feller. Just means that this is all mine. Lady?"

"Yeah, mister?"

"If you get his horse and switch his saddlebags for mine, you still earn the twenty."

"What . . . ? What you gonna do to Mr. Winters?"

"Make the punishment fit the crime."

"No!" the newspaperman gasped. Then made a gurgling sound as the razor was moved from his throat to slash a deep cut across the inside of his right wrist.

Blood bubbled up from the cut and flowed over its lips. Its dark color lightened as it became mixed with rain water.

Edge stood up, pushing the money into his hip pocket and holding out the razor, turning it this way and that, so the rain washed the blood off the blade. He raked his eyes over the shocked faces of the watchers.

"Couldn't let him get away with it," he said evenly. "I've lost too much lately."

Winters was silent now, his head craned to the side so that he could see the life-blood draining out of the artery.

"Sonofabitch, we better patch him up," George rasped. "He bleeds like that for too long, he'll be dead."

"Fitting way for a newspaperman to go, feller," the half-breed said, looking along the east stretch of the street to where the whore was leading Winters' horse back into the lighted area.

"What you say, mister?" a man asked.

"Like his paper. Died from a lousy circulation."

Chapter Five

"HEY, young feller, it looks like them comin' in now!"

Edge shifted the Stetson off his face and onto the top of his head, stood up and picked his way out of the roofless building that had once been a barrack. Halted with his Winchester canted to his left shoulder and looked across the littered former drill square. Squinted up at the point where the post's south wall met the cloudless blue sky. Saw the bearded Howie Green up there, the old-timer shielding his eyes from the noon sun as he peered toward the southwest.

The *Federale* post at Mesa del Huracan had not been used in a long time. The stone wall which enclosed it was as good as ever and looked like it could last forever. But the abode buildings were crumbling and every piece of timber used in the construction of the fort had suffered the decay of mouldering damp and bleaching sun.

So that the only way to get up on the wall was by climbing the rubble of the one time guardhouse to the right of the gateless entrance. Edge had taken that route several times since he and Green arrived at the post the previous evening, taking his turn at watching for riders out on the high plain surrounding the fort.

Now he remained on the ground, zigzagging at an unhurried pace among the rubble, to cross the square and halt in the south-facing gap.

"Off there to the right," Green called down. "I count three."

"Three's right," Edge confirmed after he had gazed

into the distance and seen the riders and horses blurred on the fringe of the shimmering heat haze.

"You mind what I told you, young feller. Don't trust them Murphies. More dangerous than a barrelful of rattlers if they get a man in a corner."

"Has to be ten times you've said that."

Maybe more Edge thought absently as he fixed his gaze on the approaching riders. The bearded old-timer had done a great deal of talking during the long, hot ride under the Sonora sun between Pueblo San Luis and here. Mostly about his hatred for bounty hunters in general and the Murphy brothers in particular. He made a lot of money out of such men. But he did business with those the bounty hunters tracked down, too. And it was obvious where his sympathies lay.

It wasn't until they reached the derelict *Federale* post at sundown the previous day that Howie Green revealed he had a personal reason for his views. He had come down to Mexico himself, five years ago, on the trail of an outlaw. But not as a bounty hunter. The fugitive was his bastard son and he had hoped to get the boy to reform.

But the boy was dead when he found him a few miles south of San Luis. Shot and robbed by the Murphy brothers, it seemed. Although there was no proof.

Green buried his son close to the church in the hills and bought the store in the village to make money to keep himself and to wait for some solid evidence that the Murphies murdered his son. There was still no evidence, but the old man was convinced in his own mind of their guilt. And if there was an opportunity to see them pay—in any way for anything—he was determined to be a witness.

Green had admitted his motive for coming here last night, as he and Edge shared a pork-and-beans meal beside a flickering fire.

Now, as the half-breed saw the trio of riders become more clearly defined in the distance, he thought of that first time the old-timer had warned him about the Murphies back in San Luis before he got drunk. Maybe as drunk as he got in Mayville Wyoming while he was trying to live with the knowledge of the way Beth died.

Beth's eyes were green. So were those of Flo Cash. Belle, the Mayville whore? He had no idea. But that link was too tenuous anyway.

He touched the shirt pocket in which the letter rested. The letter that provided a much more concrete connection to trigger memories of Beth. But even in his drunken stupor at the cantina his mind had involuntarily rejected recollections of his wife as a living, vibrant person. Instead, he had recalled that other liquor sodden time when he took the first dangerous steps toward shedding the unbearable burden of all engulfing grief.

"Hey, ain't that . . . yeah, that's an Injun they got with them!" Green yelled down from the top of the wall.

Edge steadied the Winchester with his right hand as he worked the action to pump a shell into the breech. He left the hammer cocked.

His hooded eyes never shifted from the bare-to-the-waist man who rode between Pat and Sean Murphy as he raised a hand to his shirt pocket and took out the letter. He had discarded the envelope several days ago and the piece of paper he unfolded was patched with sweat stains which made the penciled wording difficult to read. But he didn't read it, anyway. Held the letter down at his side. He knew what was written on the paper.

Joe Hedges—you want the redskin that killed your wif you cum to the Mex army fort at Mesa del Huracan on Jun 12 and me and Pat'll give you him but you got to giv us 2 grand.

"You come all this way to kill an Apache, young feller?" Green asked in an incredulous tone as he came down over the guardhouse rubble.

"A Sioux."

"A Sioux? In this part of the world?"

"Guess he's not here from choice."

Green halted beside the half-breed and peered out

through the gateway. "Even with these old eyes of mine, that's plain to see."

The brave was obviously a prisoner. He rode bareback on a burro, with ropes lashing his arms to his sides. Two other lengths of rope were noosed around his neck, their ends tied to the saddlehorns of Pat and Sean Murphy.

Because of the constant danger that their captive might fall off his mount and be choked by the nooses, the brothers maintained an easy pace. Slow, but sure. And eventually all three riders were close enough to be seen in detail.

"Sure is one sick-lookin' Injun," the old-timer growled as the Murphies reined in their horses, turning them inwards to block the burro's path.

The brave had the mark of death on him. Seen in the pitiful thinness of his naked torso and the sparseness of his gaunt face. He probably stood more than five-and-a-half foot tall but weighed no more than eighty pounds. Once he had been well built. This showed in the size of his bones and the way his dark skin sagged between them. Whether he had ever been handsome, it was impossible to see. For the folds of skin on his face, like those on his torso, were covered with festering sores and the scabs of infections which were healing. A great deal of his long black hair had fallen out leaving patches of his skull naked. His dark eyes looked to be already dead. Maybe the mind in back of them already was.

The small-of-stature men who flanked the pathetically sick Sioux Indian looked to be in fine shape. That they were brothers, it was obvious, for they were similar enough in the makeup of features on their round faces to be twins. High foreheads, broad noses, pouted mouths, small blue eyes and bulging cheeks. It was an impression they made efforts to encourage by dressing alike—in black from their hats to their boots. They even rode identical black geldings.

"I'm Patrick Murphy," the small man on the right announced from twenty feet away from where Edge

140

and Green stood in the fort entrance. "This here is me brother, Sean. And you'll be Josiah Hedges. Or Edge as they call you now."

There was a half-smile on his lips as he spoke, his voice featured with a lilting Irish accent.

"You got that right, feller."

"What you doing here, old man?" Sean asked of Green. He did not smile.

"It's a free country, ain't it?" the red-bearded man countered.

Patrick Murphy laughed and gave a gentle tug on his length of rope noosed around the brave's neck. "Not for this fine fellow, it isn't." Then all humor was gone from his stubbled face and his voice. "Why is the storekeeper here?"

Edge spat into the dust, the globule of saliva soaking into the arid ground two feet in front of him.

"He's a stranger hereabouts," Green growled. "I showed him the way. A guide, you might say."

"Is that right, Mr. Hedges?" Pat asked.

"It matter to you, feller?"

"He doesn't like us."

"Who the frig does?" Green snorted.

"Take care, old man!" Sean snarled, and dropped a hand to drape the butt of his holstered Colt.

"Leave it, brother!" Pat said quickly, sharing a scowl between Sean and the old-timer. Then he returned his attention to Edge. "In your hand? Is that the letter Sean wrote to you?"

"Right again, feller."

A nod. "Sean is not much with the writing. I'll be thinking you'll want to hear about our prisoner? How we came by him and how we know he is responsible for the passing of your wife?"

"Hell, why brother?" Sean muttered. "What I wrote brought the man down here from Paraiso, Pat.

"We are asking two thousand dollars for the Indian, brother," Pat pointed out. "Mr. Hedges must be sure he is buying the right Indian."

Howie Green had lost interest in the Murphy brothers now, intrigued by the reason that was emerging for this meeting of ill-assorted men at the isolated fort. When he looked at the half-breed he saw the same lack of expression that stirred anxiety within the minds of the slightly built brothers.

"Am I right yet again, Mr. Hedges?" Pat asked.

"Figure I ought to know why I should be grateful for small Murphies," the half-breed drawled.

Green vented one of his cackling laughs, which was curtailed by the ugly scowls that suddenly appeared on the faces of the brothers.

"We can't help the way we're made, mister!" Pat snarled. "You going to listen or not?"

"I already told you, feller."

Sean continued to smart from the comment about his size but Pat became composed, while the Indian brave between them sat the burro like a wax model fashioned in not-quite-human shape.

"We bought him from a man in El Paso," Pat explained. "Fellow called Grainger. Did you ever hear of him?"

Edge shook his head, looking at the Indian to try to catch some spark of interest in the dark eyes. There was none, the brave staring into the middle-distance.

"This Grainger, he had heard of you. Of how you lost your wife in a Sioux uprising in the Dakotas. He was a cowpuncher up there when you and your wife worked the farm. Heard how you went after the Indian who killed her and came up empty. Few months ago he was up in the Dakotas again and heard this fellow bragging in a Deadwood saloon about the way he raped your wife and killed her. It seems you are something of a legend in that part of the country."

"Why did Grainger sell him to you, feller?" Edge asked.

"Got tired of tracking you, is the way he told it," Patrick Murphy answered. "Seems you move around a lot and he never could catch up with you. Perhaps because this Indian slowed him down all the time."

"Seems to me," the half-breed said, "that a man trav-

142

eling with this brave would be traveling light."

Patrick Murphy glanced at the Indian and shrugged. "He was rather sickly when we bought him off Grainger. Sean and me, we tried to beef him up a little, but the sonofabitch won't eat."

Sean vented a snort of impatience. "Shit, we're wasting time, Pat." He fixed his stare on the face of Edge. "Grainger gave up on finding you, mister. So we bought the Indian. Took a chance because it didn't look as if he would live too long. We didn't know when you'd be next in this part of the country and we sure as hell never go far away from it. But we got lucky. Heard from a fellow that you were in Paraiso, so we fixed for that McCord kid to give you the message. That's it, mister. There's nothing more to say. You know the price. Give us two thousand and he's yours."

"What profit will that make for you fellers?"

"Our business," Sean answered shortly.

"My brother is correct, Mr. Hedges," Patrick added. "The profit will be high because the business was of a high-risk nature."

"Two thousand, uh?"

"Like the letter said."

Edge screwed the paper up into a tight ball and dropped it into the dust. "He ain't worth two cents to me."

"The hell you say!" Sean snarled and dropped a hand to drape the butt of his holstered Colt again.

The half-breed whipped the rifle down from his shoulder and streaked his right hand across the front of his belly to receive the sun-warmed barrel.

"Hold it!" Patrick yelled, scowled at his brother and then looked hard into the half-breed's lean and bristled face. "The way this Grainger fellow told the story, it sounded like the truth. And the letter brought you a lot of miles to get here. That was the reason we arranged for the meeting to be out in the middle of nowhere. Fact that you're here must mean—"

"I didn't have any appointments any place else," Edge put in evenly. "And riding down here there was as good a chance of Beth's killer getting what's coming to him as anywhere."

"What's that supposed to mean?" Patrick asked, his suspicion expanding.

"He's trying to outsmart us, Pat!" Sean growled.

From the brief flicker of interest which came and went in the dark eyes of the starving Sioux brave, Edge knew the Indian understood English.

"I asked you a question, mister!" Patrick insisted.

"I killed her, feller."

"Then why the hell did you—" Patrick started as he and Howie Green stared at the half-breed with matching expressions of incredulity.

Sean's rage, which had been simmering below the surface for so long, abruptly exploded into violent action. "All the friggin' trouble we been to!" he roared, and snatched the Colt from his holster.

Maybe he intended to vent his spite against the Indian. Or perhaps Edge. Even Howie Green. Certainly his frustration demanded an outlet of lethal proportions. But his gun was not aimed at any living thing when the brave lunged to the side, thudding his shoulder into the crook of Sean Murphy's neck.

"Pat!" the man shrieked as he was knocked from the saddle.

"Look out!" Green yelled.

Instinctively, the half-breed tracked the rifle to follow the course of the brother with a gun in his hand.

Seeing this, Patrick Murphy suspected the worse, drew his own revolver and blasted a shot at Edge. But his aim was spoiled by a movement of his mount, the horse reacting to the jerking rope between saddlehorn and the neck of the Indian.

Edge felt the tug as a bullet tunneled into and out of the crown of his hat. He dropped into a crouch and tracked the rifle barrel back again, away from the falling Sean, across the Indian in process of toppling from the burro, and at Patrick.

Patrick thumbed back the hammer of his revolver.

Edge squeezed the trigger of the Winchester. His bullet took Patrick in the chest, left of center, blasted a hole through his heart and exited at the back in a splash of crimson. The bullet's victim did a backward somersault out of the saddle and crashed to the ground in a billow of dust.

Perhaps the Sioux brave was already dead by then, his neck broken by the suden tautening of the rope. Certainly he was dead a moment later when Patrick's horse reared and turned to raise the bound Indian up off the ground and over the back of the burro. Then both horses and the burro bolted, the lifeless form of the brave looking like a bundle of old clothes as it was dragged along under the swirling dust erupted by pumping hooves.

"Don't shoot me, don't shoot me!" Sean Murphy shrieked.

This as the impassive Edge looked at him and aimed the Winchester at him, saw him kneeling on the ground in the settling dust-cloud, hands clasped in front of his chest as if praying.

"Don't listen to him!" Green shrieked. "Blast the sonofabitch to hell, the murderin' bastard."

"If he killed anyone, it ain't nothing to me," the half-breed drawled, and canted the rifle back to his shoulder.

He started to turn away, then did a double-take. The dust motes had almost all settled now. He could see Sean's Colt lying on the ground—out of reach of the man. But the matching gun which had spun out of Patrick's hand was nowhere to be seen.

Sean began to get to his feet, lips and limbs quivering. Hands down now. Too far down. His shoulders were hunched as he reached between his thighs.

"No," he whimpered as he realized the slitted blue eyes of the half-breed had spotted his play.

But he was committed to the act of bringing out, leveling and firing his brother's ready-cocked revolver.

And uttered his final plea with a tone of hopelessness, as he saw a blur of a movement—the right hand of Edge streaking to the holster and drawing the Colt.

The last thing he saw was the spurt of smoke from

the muzzle of the revolver. Then he was sprawled out on his back, blood pumping out of his heart to spread a great stain across his shirt front.

"Sneaky!" Green yelled. "Didn't I tell you them Murphys were sneaky!"

Edge returned the gun to the holster and gazed bleakly out to where the two horses and the burro had finally come to a halt.

"But then you ain't exactly . . . I don't know what," the old-timer growled, scratching his bald head as he looked at the half-breed. "Comin' all the way down here from across the border on what you knowed was a fool's errand from the start."

Edge spat into the dust, took off his hat and prodded a finger into one of the two holes in the crown.

"You really kill your wife, young feller?"

"Way I see it, I did."

"But you ain't gonna tell me about it?"

"It's a long story, feller. Already on the record."

Green shrugged, then looked at the corpses of the Murphy brothers and asked, "You mind if I don't leave them like that?"

"Suit yourself," Edge replied and moved back through the gateway into the fort.

While he saddled his horse, mounted and rode across the debris-littered drill square, he heard a series of thudding sounds, accompanied by a snarling, repetitive monologue by the old-timer.

"There you bastard! I knowed you killed my boy! I just wished you could feel this! There you bastard! You killed him! For sure you killed him! On account of you, I ain't got a kin in the world! You killed him. Take that, you bastard!"

Gradually, he became breathless. The venom went out of his voice and the thudding sounds were less frenetic.

As Edge rode out through the gateway, he was in time to see Green stagger from the body of Sean to that of Patrick, the old man's pants legs splashed with blood erupted from the caved-in, almost fleshless-face of the first brother he had stomped. Then, as the half-breed watched, Howie Green began to thud a boot heel down onto the unfeeling head of Patrick, his actions and words as forceful as at the start now that he had a fresh target at which to direct his revenge.

For two minutes he kept it up, reducing the face of Patrick to the same gruesome pulp as that which made Sean unrecognizable. Then he was through and he reeled away, made it to the side of the gateway before exhaustion caught up with him and he sagged against the wall and slid down it.

"Sorry, young feller," he gasped as some of the flies he had disturbed at the corpses settled on his blood-stained pants cuffs. "But it was somethin' I felt I just had to do."

Edge nodded. "Like me, coming down here. No sweat."

Green raised his head and managed to spread a grin of satisfaction across his ancient face. "Least I got somethin' out of all this." Then he scowled toward the corpses with bloodied heads. "See them yellow punks pay the price for what they done to my boy."

Edge looked at the dead brothers with cold eyes that perhaps, just for a moment, showed a glimmer of pity. "They bought it sure enough, feller," he muttered. "But it was a lousy deal. With or without Green stamps."

More bestselling western adventure from Pinnacle, America's #1 series publisher. Over 4 million copies of EDGE in print!